THE *Mind* OF A
REVOLUTION

FROM RESISTANCE TO REVOLT

THE *Mind* OF A REVOLUTION

FROM RESISTANCE TO REVOLT

CAM MOLINEUX

ISBN (Ebook): 979-8-218-91271-0
ISBN (Paperback): 979-8-218-91270-3

Dedicated to those who bring history to life,

and

in memory of Edmund Pendleton, who helped create it.

I am for peace, but when I speak, they are for war.

—Psalm 120:7 (NASB)

Contents

Author's Note

History is messy. In 1774, uncertainties ran rampant. Many of our Founding Fathers struggled with various concerns. Was war really necessary? And if it came, what would it mean for loved ones? Disagreements among colonists left leaders to weigh each vote they cast, both locally and in Philadelphia.

We benefit from hindsight and are tempted to read history as if colonists knew the outcome. The war would last for years, many would die, but in the end, America would throw off the chains of tyranny which threatened to bind her. But for those who lived through it, decisions often came after years of struggle.

I invite you to come along as we explore one such journey, the pilgrimage of Edmund Pendleton, my 7x great uncle. In Virginia's House of Burgesses, his colleagues looked to this kind, warmhearted soul for leadership. He was wise, thoughtful, and slow to change. I am proud of the care he took as he considered the consequences of war but also of his eventual decision to help point the colonies toward independence.

In my first novel, which ends where this one picks up (1774), you'll explore a city alive with action—action which pushes colonists to consider war with their Motherland as a viable option. Both stories are true, with pieces of fiction woven in to help them flow. Yet they are worlds apart.

In America's largest and most respected colony, the wheels of change turn slowly. In this cautious place, the growing debate forces Edmund Pendleton, Patrick Henry, and others to wrestle with *The Mind of a Revolution*.

CHAPTER 1

My Caroline County Forest

March – April 1774

Edmund Pendleton sat by the bed of his ailing wife, caressing her feverish hand with his cool one. The crackling fire in the corner hearth pushed away the late winter chill. Snow clouds filtered the light coming in from one of the dormer windows.

Lord, please don't take her from me. I don't know if I could bear another loss.

The worst of the fever had given way to rest. A good sign, the doctor said.

"Sarah," Pendleton whispered, "it's been thirty good years together, and I don't want them to end now."

Please, Lord. I'm trusting you for her healing.

Pendleton leaned back in his chair, wishing her well-being could consume his attention. He closed his eyes. Boston's misconduct, dumping tea into their harbor, could not be ignored. He would debate the issue with Virginia's other county representatives in Williamsburg soon enough, but for now—

A soft rap came at the door.

Pendleton lifted his eyes. "Come in."

The door creaked open, and in stepped a woman with enough flesh on her bones to guard against the bite of winter. The white apron accentuated her ebony skin.

"Colonel Pendleton, sorry ta bother you, with the missis and all, but Johnny—er, Jack—is in the liberry. Says he finished the errand you asked him to do."

Pendleton smiled. "He will always be little Johnny Taylor to us, won't he, Cloe?"

"Yass, suh." The housemaid bobbed her head in agreement.

The man turned his gaze back to his sleeping wife. "Please tell him I will be down soon."

The scent of books, both old and new, could revive Pendleton's spirit like no other, as could the presence of the nephew he had raised as his own after Jack's father died. "Can I get you anything? Something warm to drink?"

Jack lifted his tall, lean body from the chair that he pushed under the library's grand table, which filled much of the room. "No, thank you." His brow wrinkled above his deep-set eyes, and he tipped his head toward the stairs. "How is she?"

"We hope she has turned a corner, but time alone will tell. She is resting now."

"And you?" Jack asked. "You look weary."

Pendleton stared into the nothingness beyond the young man. "I don't mind telling you, her illness has touched a wound deep inside me. But I am grateful that many are seeing that my physical needs are well taken care of. And my soul finds rest in the Lord."

Jack's focus dropped to the documents scattered on the table.

"Cloe tells me you completed your mission," Pendleton said.

Jack picked up one of the papers. "It was not the easiest assignment you've ever given me. The location of each courthouse record isn't etched on the palm of my hand, like it is on yours." He passed the document to Pendleton.

Pendleton scanned the land survey. "Very good. The property dispute has become ugly, and this is just what we need to help settle the case. I expect your work as an attorney to blossom in this county."

"I learned from the best." Jack swept his hand toward the shelves lining the wall. "Like Colonel Jefferson, I'm envious of your library. It served well as my schoolroom, but I will miss it when I am no longer living under your roof."

Pendleton returned the paper to the table, then walked over and pulled a worn volume off the shelf. "Start early like I did, and you'll be surprised how it grows. At sixteen, I took my first job as clerk of the vestry." Pendleton thumbed through the pages, then let the book fall open in his hands. "After three years as an apprentice, I had fallen in love with all things law." A gentle laugh spilled from his lips. "Not for everyone, I know. But surrounded by Major Robinson's rapport with the people, and there were plenty of legal minds who passed through the courthouse in those days, it hardly seemed like work."

"And your library?"

"I used the money from the job at the church to purchase my first books. I apprenticed with Major Robinson by day and studied at night." He closed the book, laid it on the table, and tapped it. "This was among my first. Since Latin punctuated the county records, learning that language consumed my attention from the start. Not too bad, I suppose, for someone who had very little formal education."

"Everyone admires you," Jack said. "I know that firsthand."

"God has blessed me with many friends, and I don't believe I have done anything to provoke those who aren't. But I am afraid that in this line of work, we will always have a few adversaries." Pendleton put his hand on Jack's shoulder. "Thank you for obtaining these records. Now if you will excuse me, I will check on your Aunt Sarah, then get back to the business at hand. If all is well, we can catch up on more family news at the upcoming gathering. Cloe has been busier than a momma bird getting ready for spring. The ballroom will be spotless in time for our Easter celebration."

With April came a focus on the resurrection. Tunes flowing from a violin provided the ballroom with a soothing background while more than twenty kinfolk chatted about anything and everything. The winter weather would soon lose its hold, if Mother Nature would but catch a glimpse of the calendar.

With his wife seated by his side, Pendleton's view from the room's perimeter left him beaming from ear to ear. "I thank the Lord every day that you recovered from your illness. Last month was troublesome, and I'm grateful the page has turned to a healthier time."

He squeezed his lady's hand. She squeezed back, her eyes reflecting the love between them.

Their heads swayed with the music for several minutes, then Pendleton nodded toward the chandelier. Light from its candles fluttered against the finery of the womenfolk as the beaus moved them along in step with the rhythm. "Remember when we added this wing?"

Neck-length curls brushed against Sarah's collar. "At the time, it felt like an extravagance, but oh, the memories it holds."

Pendleton felt a tug on his breeches.

"Papa." The wee voice grabbed at Pendleton's heart every time, especially coming from one of Junior's children. Although through his nephew, Edmund's name would live on for years to come.

He reached down and pulled the tot onto his knee, then flashed a grin at Sarah. "Perhaps the Lord didn't provide us with offspring of our own, but he made our quiver full, nonetheless."

"Most everyone is here," Sarah said. "Jack, Edmund Jr., and even John Penn, along with his family. I hear their home in North Carolina is just about ready."

At the mention of John Penn, Pendleton began to fidget with one of the buttons on his waistcoat. "If the aromas from the kitchen are any indication, Scipio has outdone herself once again."

Sarah patted her husband's free knee. "Listen to me, Edmund. John loves you, as you love him. The differences between you cannot lessen that."

Pendleton nodded, bouncing one knee.

The little one giggled and clapped his hands. "Mo, mo."

"John is still finding his place in the world," Sarah said. "He is barely thirty years old. Give him time. Perhaps he will come around."

"They mean everything to me, each one of them." The toddler shuffled down from Pendleton's knee and scurried away. Pendleton chuckled. "They bring joy to my life. Most of the time." He stared across the room. "But next month's meeting in Williamsburg. Oh, my."

"Challenges await?"

The hands of the longcase clock across the room reflected the hour. Pendleton pushed himself to his feet and turned to his wife. "The news from Boston will provide plenty of kindling for a lively debate amongst the burgesses. You know I would rather stay here in my Caroline County forest with you, my dear. I will enjoy it while I can, before duty comes and whisks me away." He placed one arm across his waist, bowed, then extended his other hand to Sarah. "In the meantime, I would welcome the pleasure of your company over what promises to be a most scrumptious feast."

CHAPTER 2

Boston's Plea

MAY 26 - MID-JUNE 1774

The chill that filled the second-story council chambers went beyond the frosty May, which had every plantation owner on edge. The field hands would need to reckon with the endangered crops back home while Pendleton dealt with matters of the colony in Williamsburg. Candles flickered atop brass sconces dotting the walls between windows reaching to the ceiling and running down each side of the sizable room. A gilded frame hung at one end, displaying a portrait of King William III, for whom the city was named.

Pendleton studied the somber expressions of the hundred men standing three deep around the perimeter of the room—men who had been abruptly summoned by Virginia's royal governor. Though expected, his call arrived too soon for the burgesses to complete the business entrusted to them. The public would suffer as a result of the swiftness with which Patrick Henry and others had insisted they debate the more controversial matters.

Fellow burgesses, several still in their forties, shuffled in front of

Pendleton, vying for comfortable positions, then an accidental bump from the gentleman in front of him almost sent him toppling. Grabbing the coattails in front of him prevented a tumble to the floor.

"Oh, my." One of the gentlemen spun around to catch him. "Colonel Pendleton, forgive me." He stepped aside and extended his hand toward the front row. "Please, sir, come forward to your rightful place."

Pendleton nodded a thank-you to the young man and slid to the front row before surveying the scene playing out before them.

The royal governor, Lord Dunmore, stood at the head of the mammoth table, his rusty-red hair a good match for his impetuous nature. He clutched the paper notice whose jagged tear on the top edge indicated it had been ripped from a tree somewhere in town. While the choice of words could have been more thoughtfully chosen, the sentiments of the public declaration should have been enough to keep the governor's anger at bay. Yet, as the king's representative, he must fulfill his duty. The crumpled paper in Lord Dunmore's hand left no question that the House of Burgesses had crossed the line by declaring a day of fasting, humiliation, and prayer. Henry's posse referring to the situation in Boston as a "hostile invasion" during their shortened session had added to the list of things the governor could not ignore.

His Scottish complexion flushed a deep pink as he waved the broadside at them. "Gentlemen, referring to Massachusetts Bay as your sister colony reeks of a desire to form your own government."

Pendleton closed his eyes. Nothing could be further from the desires of most of the gentlemen circled around their governor. Pendleton opened his eyes and caught a glimpse of Patrick Henry who represented the handful of those in the minority. Did he understand the stir he and his followers had caused? The unnecessary confusion they had incited?

"Your actions," Lord Dunmore's voice thundered, "mimic those who, in days gone by, were responding to threats of invasion or of civil war. Gentlemen, no such threat is upon you."

Pendleton furrowed his brow. Perhaps if the document's author had crafted his words with more consideration, would the governor's fury have been kept at bay?

The governor glared at the men before him. "Yet the terms contained in the paper I hold in my hand, which was published by order of the House, make it necessary for me to dissolve you. You are dissolved accordingly."

The declaration resounded deep within Pendleton's chest. The harsh announcement brought an official end to this session of the assembly. Until the governor decided otherwise, the burgesses would not meet, leaving the people of Virginia without a voice in their own government. Pendleton shot a glance toward Peyton Randolph, one of only two burgesses with more seniority than he and an heir to Virginia's wealth and power. As the Speaker of the House, surely Randolph would have a response for the governor. Their eyes met, but the silent communication between them made it clear none would be given. Pendleton dipped his chin. The governor's wrath demanded a gentle answer in order to keep hopes alive for future sessions. Previous spats with the royal governor paled in comparison with this episode.

The world had changed.

Possibly forever.

The next day, Pendleton found a spot among his fellow delegates in the Apollo Room of the Raleigh Tavern, just beyond the shadows of the Capitol. The clash with Lord Dunmore had pushed the now-homeless burgesses to find a new meeting place. Servants weaved in and out of the nearly hundred men, doing what they could to adapt the twenty-by-forty-foot space for the impromptu meeting. Tables had been pushed aside and additional chairs brought in. Refreshments sat untouched amid the heated debate that centered around how to respond to Parliament's harsh treatment of Boston. Pendleton tugged at his collar. Perhaps the exceptionally cool spring had become a blessing.

Rumors around town claimed the day of prayer had been a political move cooked up by Thomas Jefferson, Patrick Henry, and a handful of others in order to incite the masses. Nonetheless, prayers would be lifted up all around Virginia to the Sovereign Lord on the first day of June, just four days hence, and in tandem with Britain blockading Boston's port. Would the prayers for Boston come too late for the drama unfolding before him today?

A proposed document denouncing Parliament's plan to shut down Boston's harbor provided focus for the deliberations. Pendleton collected his thoughts, then rose from his chair. A calm came over the room as all eyes turned to the wise and gentle leader. "The proposed opening line of the document must stay. If we are anything, we are his Majesty's most dutiful and loyal subjects. Not following blindly, as some would suggest, but with the honor and respect that our Motherland deserves."

Many nodded.

Patrick Henry scrambled to his feet. "Boston has sought redress for her grievances from the Motherland for how many years now? And to what avail? To have their port closed to trade?"

With a slight nod, Pendleton acknowledged Henry's concerns, then expressed his own. "It is indeed an attack upon our constitutional rights for Parliament to send troops to intervene in the destruction of private property. The stench it leaves suggests it was a preconcerted scheme that produced the consequences for which they wished."

Another burgess chimed in. "Personal property or not, the tax on tea without our consent is an assault on our liberties. We must be bold in our response."

Several men tapped their walking sticks against the floorboards in protest.

"Bold, yet wise," Pendleton said before returning to his chair and silently petitioning heaven. *Lord, please give me wisdom to know how to point the way to redress through more peaceful means.* The newspaper had certainly done no good by printing a piece indicating a bloody war might be the answer. Had no thought been given to the consequences of such views?

Richard Henry Lee, gifted with both his tongue and pen, stood, his cheeks and broad forehead flush with emotion. "The proposed embargo against the East India Company is not enough. Yes, they are the ones who shipped the tea, with its detestable taxes, to our ports. But we must demand that the embargo extend to *every* item coming to or going from our shores. Only that will provide enough pain for our Motherland to undo the harm she has inflicted upon Boston and prevent her from doing the same for all of Britain's colonies."

Henry, still standing from his previous pronouncement, raised a fist. "Mr. Lee has spoken well. You may have heard of the recent letter he received from his brother in London, which reveals Britain's refusal to listen to our pleas for redress—until we fall at her feet."

Pendleton glanced around. Many in the room leaned forward in their chairs, eyes opened wide, as Henry continued.

"Or the news that they now refer to us as turkeys whose wings must be clipped. Does this sound like a kingdom who sees us as fellow citizens? I think not."

Lord, help us.

The former Speaker of the House of Burgesses stood and pivoted toward the majority of the men surrounding him. "Gentlemen, it has been a long and grueling debate," Randolph said, "and despite these late words by Messrs. Henry and Lee, the general consent has become apparent. Out of tender regard for our fellow merchants and manufacturers in Britain, we will refrain from a more general embargo, which would be of great harm to those who might not have been involved in inflicting pain upon our sister colony. A document will be available later today for those who wish to sign it and, in so doing, join the association and agree to more limited restrictions on trade."

A smile tugged at the corners of Pendleton's lips. Reason would prevail.

"Many more discussions need to take place," Randolph continued, "and will indeed happen within the newly-formed group when the time seems appropriate." He looked at Pendleton, Henry, and a few others. "In the meantime, our Committee of Correspondence will communicate with other colonies about our desire for an annual meeting of a general congress to deliberate on these and others issues that may arise.

"As you know, ramifications of Britain's actions reach far beyond the boundaries of Massachusetts, thus every colony needs to be involved in any decisions made. Thankfully, they know to look to us as the largest colony and oldest legislature on these shores, to help guide the way. Once the committee receives a response to our recommendation for a general congress, you can expect to hear from us as to the next step. May God be with us all as we sail into uncharted waters."

The meeting came to a close, and Pendleton lifted himself from his chair and made his way to the other members of the committee already beginning to gather. "I know many of you are anxious to get home," Pendleton said. "And if a meeting of the colonies is to take place before year's end, time is of the essence."

Servants helped pull chairs around a single table, and provided paper, pen, and ink.

Pendleton settled in, then turned his attention to the others seated around the table. "Gentlemen, shall we get started?"

With only twenty-five representatives seated around the large table, the Apollo Room provided more elbow room than it had a couple days before. Pendleton sighed. Boston's plea for help had arrived in Williamsburg soon after the Committee of Correspondence sent letters to the other colonies. With the situation in Boston escalating, that city's desire to draw other colonies into the conflict were moving events toward an alarming crisis. Surely the next day's fasting and prayer would be gladly observed.

Twenty-five had been all Randolph, the moderator, could gather to discuss the latest packet of information. Before returning to their respective counties, the other delegates, along with most local merchants, had signed the agreement. The newly-formed Virginia Association stood on firm ground.

Richard Henry Lee paced around the room. With sixteen years in the House of Burgesses, he had a deep well of knowledge from which to draw. "It is doubtful we can trust Lord Dunmore's claim that things will be settled in Boston."

Colonel George Washington, who had entered as a burgess the same year as Lee, leaned in. "Especially since the pledge originated with General Gage. He has not been kind to the New England province he was sent to 'protect.'" Washington's towering frame, coupled with experience in the war against the French and Indians, commanded attention wherever he went.

Randolph nodded and lifted his large frame from the chair. "So, it is agreed that we will summon the others back to Williamsburg to discuss Boston's request to cease all trade with Great Britain?"

Pendleton joined the others in sending up sounds of affirmation.

"Then I will see you again on the first of August," Randolph said. "This will allow two months for you to collect a sense of those in your respective counties. Too, it will provide opportunity to check on your businesses, crops, and loved ones. Godspeed to you all."

Pendleton leaned back in the rocker and barely noticed the squeak emitting from the floorboards of his front porch. While being away from the clamor of Williamsburg had its benefits, his two weeks at home had come with its own set of issues. The June breeze brushing his face, he gazed down at the visitor standing at the foot of the stairs. The joy John Penn had brought to him over the years now mingled with sadness. "Although Parliament has made several missteps in recent years," Pendleton said, "we must be wise in how we respond. Otherwise, the matter will escalate beyond what any of us can imagine."

Penn blinked against the sun beginning to break through the morning fog, revealing the shadowy figures already moving about the vast plantation. "But isn't ten years of attempts at peace more than enough time to settle our differences with the Motherland?"

"For someone, such as yourself, who is barely a decade into adulthood, it would seem so. But things of great importance, and with great consequences if not handled with wisdom and care, often take time to resolve. We owe our Motherland a great deal." Pendleton studied the paint peeling off the arm of his rocking chair. A weight settled on his heart before he turned his attention back to Penn. "Then your decision is final?"

"I am afraid it is," Penn said. "You have taught me well, and for that I am forever grateful. But in this matter we must part ways. While Virginia wrestles with how to respond to the situation in Boston, I believe North Carolina will provide a safe haven for me and my views."

Calls from a flock of birds flying overhead gave both men pause, then Pendleton continued. "Take care of your bride, and give your children a hug for me. Heaven knows they'll be missed." So many years invested in this young man, and now this. What words could he provide to convince his protégé to return to the more honorable path? Words that would encourage, not push away? Pendleton stood, took two steps forward, then fixed his eyes on Penn. "I am afraid casting your lot with Boston will only lead to troublesome times."

"You taught me to do the right thing, no matter the cost." Penn stared at the ground for a moment. "I believe in the path I have chosen."

"I only hope you will not live to regret the decision you have made," Pendleton said. "You have been like a son to me. I am proud of the man you have become. Old habits die hard, yet you have outgrown your given name. From this day forward, when in the presence of others, I will refer to you as Mr. Penn."

Pendleton's paternal spirit rose within him. "John, look at me."

The young man lifted his head.

"As you go out into the world," Pendleton said, "don't forget to speak up. Those of us who know you well may be able to surmise what you are trying to say despite your habit of whispering, but others may not. Differing views aside, we love you and want others to get to know the wonderful man you have become."

Something within Pendleton ached. If only they had more time together during these uncertain days. Surely the frail young man standing before him would do well in the company of his closer kin. Yet rumors regarding the political undercurrents of the area in which they had settled gave reason for concern. "Please give my greetings to your dear mother when you arrive. Let her know her family here is doing as well as to be expected under the present circumstances. Tell her I am taking good care of our grandfather's plantation. God rest his soul."

"She speaks of you kindly when she recounts your taking me in after the loss of my father." Penn's eyes reflected the love the two men shared but seldom expressed.

"Please send word when you arrive." Pendleton's lip quivered, and he held out his arm. "Come here, son."

Penn leapt onto the porch, and the two men embraced.

Sorrow enveloped Pendleton before he collected himself. He pushed the lad away, gripped his shoulders, and looked him square in the eyes. "You will always have a home here."

The pain of the departure now reflected in Penn's countenance. "I know. North Carolina is a week's journey, but I am hopeful I will be able to return from time to time."

"I will look forward to it."

Penn turned his gaze to the porch floorboards. "When will the burgesses return to Williamsburg?"

"In less than two months. The first of August. It is more important than ever that we burgesses represent the people of our respective counties so their voices are heard."

Penn nodded. "I must be on my way, lest my lady begins to worry."

"May God's grace shine upon you and your family as you travel together to a new life."

The young man sauntered down the steps, hesitated for a moment, then began to walk away.

Pendleton provided a slight smile when Penn cast a parting glance back at Edmundsbury, the plantation where Pendleton had done his best to mold him into a man who could take on the world. His eyes followed the lad. "Please, Lord, teach him the value of seeking a peaceful resolution." He sighed. *And the pitfalls of not giving harmony a chance.*

CHAPTER 3

Redress or Revolution?
July 14 - August 31, 1774

Pendleton stood on the stoop outside the courthouse, waving his hand at the cloud of dust kicked up by freeholders and inhabitants of Caroline County who had gathered for the rally. In the month since Penn's departure, Pendleton had continued to prepare for the unknown. Tending to legal matters of his profession and assuring the plantation was ready for his possible extended time away had kept him occupied. On this day, however, other matters demanded his attention.

Songs of liberty and scattered conversations had faded when he had taken to the stage and begun his address several minutes before. He suppressed the urge to rub his hand against his throat, sore from speaking without the use of a sounding board. Richard Bland, his friend and fellow burgess, cast Pendleton an empathetic smile from where he stood at the edge of the crowd.

"In conclusion," Pendleton said, "I would like to thank you for sharing your thoughts with me during this process. As always, my desire is to reflect the sentiments of those I represent."

"We love you, Colonel Pendleton!" someone shouted.

Pendleton lifted a hand in acknowledgement. "Thank you for allowing me the opportunity to serve you these many years. Now, I present to you our county clerk."

The clerk ascended the steps as Pendleton came down.

"Hear ye, hear ye," the clerk proclaimed. "I will read to you the instructions Caroline County has provided to Edmund Pendleton and his nephew James Taylor. Both are late burgesses who will now represent Caroline County at Virginia's Convention in Williamsburg beginning the first day of August, two-and-a-half weeks hence."

Already familiar with the words, as he had penned them himself, Pendleton motioned for Bland to follow him to the back of the crowd. They slithered through and found shade under a large oak tree, relief from the midsummer sun. The clerk's voice would drown out any private exchanges between the two men.

Pendleton held one hand under an elbow of the aging Bland as they dodged tree roots rippling across the ground's surface. Once assured of Bland's comfort, Pendleton resumed their chat from before his address to the crowd.

"It is not my livelihood I seek to protect," Pendleton said. "Heaven knows I could use less time at the courthouse, but closing them hurts the people we seek to serve. While debtors rejoice, those to whom they owe money struggle, while others cannot even file a Last Will and Testament or register a deed. I must continue to push for the courts to reopen so that I might serve those in my jurisdiction."

"You are still busy with the Robinson estate?"

"I owe so much of my success to him and his uncle." A weariness crept into Pendleton's voice. "After eight years, it seems the web has become more, not less, tangled. A list of those not caught up in John Robinson's affairs might be shorter than one of those who were. If only Virginia had never allowed the Speaker of the House to also be in charge of its treasury . . ."

Pendleton swatted at a fly, then leaned back against the tree. "But enough of that. Should I assume May's late frost and the current drought have ruined the peach crops in your county as it has in ours?"

Bland nodded.

"At least our wheat crop has miraculously—"

The throng erupted in response to the reading coming from the courthouse steps. "Hurrah!"

"No taxation without our consent!" the crowd cheered.

Pendleton grinned and extended an arm toward his friend. "Mr. Bland, I believe that paragraph is a tribute to your role in all of this."

Bland bowed his salt-and-pepper head of hair in acknowledgement. "I merely put in writing what many already believed."

The back of the crowd parted, and a lad of ten or eleven emerged from the mass of humanity. He spotted the duo, darted toward them, and lifted a hat already filled with money. "Colonel Pendleton?"

Pendleton mouthed an apology to Bland for the interruption, then reached into his waistcoat pocket, returning his attention to the lad.

"We are—"

"I know," Pendleton said as he placed his donation into the hat. "Taking up a collection for Boston. You are doing a good deed, son. I trust your family has enjoyed its most recent cup of tea. It may be the last we permit until the Motherland comes around."

The boy bobbed his head, then dashed off to be about his duty.

Words coming from the clerk gave Pendleton pause. He tapped Bland's arm, then held a finger to his own lips. "I think you'll want to hear this."

The men squared their posture as they gave their attention to the county clerk, whose voice echoed above the heads of the crowd.

"'That the African trade is injurious to this colony,'" the clerk read, "'obstructs our population by freeman, manufacturers, and others who would emigrate from Europe and settle here, and occasions an annual balance of trade against the country. Therefore, the purchase of all imported slaves ought to be united against.'"

The two men shared a moment of silence before Pendleton spoke. "When will we be rid of this evil that has plagued us for generations?"

"The irony seems to lie in those who speak of freedom," Bland said, "while leaving those who serve them in chains."

Pendleton nodded. "Dare I say the matter is even more complex than the Robinson estate?"

"Yet whispers of freedom and of independence from Britain fall from the lips of some who walk the streets in several of our colonies."

Pendleton's eyes connected with Bland's. "Freedom from tyranny, yes. But there is no reason to speak of independence from the Motherland. A redress of grievances is what we need, not a revolution of government."

Bland motioned toward the clerk. "Then you stand by the words in the instructions to defend the rights of King George?"

"Those are the desires of my constituents and I will serve them the best I can. Yet, as the instructions state, if anyone—the king or anyone else—attempts to deprive us of our just rights, he will be considered an enemy to us all. Likewise for anyone who goes about with words of independence on his lips."

"But what of Parliament altering the charter of Massachusetts Bay?"

"I agree the powers Britain has given to their new military governor, both over the judiciary and the town meetings, are unreasonable," Pendleton said. "Yet economic pressure, not threats of independence, must first be explored. The people of Britain will help us convince Parliament of the error of her ways. Besides, General Gage himself expects everything to be settled in Boston in an amicable manner in a very short time."

Bland shrugged. "Perhaps, but delegates from other counties, including Patrick Henry, may not have your patience. I've heard that Frederick County burned an effigy of the general."

"Such things lead to mindless actions and do not serve the people," Pendleton said. "There are real merits to my arguments, which I hope to present when we gather in Williamsburg in a couple of weeks."

Pendleton patted the bundle of necessities on the merchant's counter in Williamsburg. "You will include a note simply stating these are from a friend who cares?"

"I will write the note myself," the merchant said.

Pendleton sauntered to the door.

"You are a good man, Colonel Pendleton."

He turned back to the merchant, who was grinning from ear to ear.

"I am simply passing along the goodness the Lord has given to me." Pendleton bowed his head in gratitude as he opened the door and stepped out to Duke of Gloucester Street. The chatter in the capital's byways made it clear. With Dunmore away, everyone was freer to express differing opinions.

"Colonel Pendleton." The voice came from a few stores up.

Pendleton turned to see Richard Henry Lee making his way toward him. "Good to see you, Mr. Lee."

"Likewise," Lee said. "I have just arrived and am hopeful you know where we might be meeting."

"Lord Dunmore has gone to the Ohio Country. He left three weeks ago, so we should be fine to meet in the Capitol. We are after all, still the House. A rose by any other name . . ."

Lee's brow wrinkled. "Is Lord Dunmore attempting to end the war with the Shawnee singlehandedly?"

"Perhaps," Pendleton said. "The delegates from beyond the Blue Ridge will not be able to attend this week."

"I assume you are lodging at the Randolph home."

"Yes. I had business to tend to so arrived a couple days ago." Pendleton squinted at the coach coming up the street. "Is that Colonel Washington?"

Lee turned to see, then a smile eased wide across his face. "I know of none other with such beautiful beasts."

"They're stately, aren't they?"

Washington nodded a greeting as he rolled by.

"Mr. Lee," Pendleton said, "I must be about my business, but I am sure Mr. Randolph would not mind if I mentioned that your name is among those he would like to invite for a meal while we are all in town. Colonel Washington is another."

"I would be delighted."

"Then I will pass along your acceptance and look forward to seeing you at the Capitol first thing on Monday. Good day, Mr. Lee." Pendleton gave a slight bow to the gentleman with whom he was sure to clash in the days ahead. Only the Lord above knew how the week would unfold.

With six days of meetings behind them, Pendleton, Bland, Washington, and a half dozen other delegates met at Peyton Randolph's home for a parting meal. Pendleton continued to savor aromas from the mostly-devoured orange duck still filling the room. Although grateful that the Randolphs had once again opened their home to him for lodging, the gathering would make for another late night. Nonetheless, his bags were all but ready for the eighty-mile journey back to Caroline.

A warm August breeze trickled through the room's large windows, leaving the fireplace, with its stately andirons and marble mantle, as nothing more than an accent. The silver candlesticks on the table complemented the gold-laced mirrors hanging on one of the two outside walls. House servants scattered about the perimeter of the room stood ready to assist while the gentlemen seated around the table enjoyed the victuals spread out before them. The room provided a comfortable setting to continue the undying debates from the convention.

Richard Henry Lee, one of the few radicals in today's group, pushed forward with his case. "But what if the rumors that London will annihilate the assemblies of all colonies and take away our right of representation are not baseless chatter?"

The face of John Randolph, Virginia's attorney general and brother to the host, turned a deep red. "I make no pretense to be anything but loyal to the Crown. And to refer to someone as a patriot simply because he enjoys the acclamations of the people is sheer nonsense."

Recognizing the thinly veiled attack on Patrick Henry, a few of the gentlemen shifted in their chairs.

John Randolph rose from his seat and took two steps back from the table, brushing aside the servant's helping hand. "Those running the race of popularity, whilst they are the greatest sticklers for the liberties of others, are themselves the most wretched slaves in politics."

"Hear, hear!" one of his allies cried.

Pendleton tipped his head in agreement to John Randolph, whose recent pamphlet had stirred the pot.

"I will make my appeal to the rational part of the public, not to the ignorant and vulgar who are unable to manage the reins of government." John Randolph paced the room. "If you will allow me but one more thought, I will rein in my fury and permit others to express their views. 'Tis only this: If the colonists will but condemn Boston's destruction of the tea and return to quietly cultivating our soil, Parliament will welcome any petition we might send to them regarding the restoration of peace, if that petition is prepared in a language suited to the ears of princes." He turned his head to the servant who hastened to his side and helped him back into his chair.

Pendleton's fingers tingled at the thought of drafting such a plea.

Lee leaned into the table. "With all due respect, Mr. Randolph, those of us who see things differently do not believe that merely opening the eyes of those whom we serve is an act of rebellion."

Washington, quiet for much of the meal, stirred. "Yet, if needed, no one should hesitate for a moment to take up arms in defense of liberty."

Pendleton touched his napkin to his lips, then laid it aside. "Gentlemen, I agree with much of what has been said, yet believe we must return our focus to the arguments of the case rather than spend our time quarreling amongst ourselves."

Peyton Randolph perked up. "Please, Colonel Pendleton, would you be so kind as to outline those for us. I believe the reminders will do us all some good."

"Of course," Pendleton said.

Peyton Randolph nodded to one of the servants, setting a chain of activities into motion.

As they removed empty plates from the table and replaced them with the final course, Pendleton began. "With the delectable treat set before us, I see my competition is great."

The men nodded as they dipped their spoons into the chocolate pudding.

"First and foremost," Pendleton said, "we must remember we are here to represent, and dare I say protect, those who sent us. While not every line of instruction from one county aligns with those from another, we embrace John Locke's revolutionary principles, including our willingness to concede authority to the government if their conduct protects the public good.

"Too, I need not remind you that death is a price we must not pay lightly. At times, it is called for, and the war with France, barely a decade past, hangs heavy upon those who lost loved ones."

At the reminder of those losses, a hush settled over the gathering.

Washington's words broke into the silence. "When lives are at stake, we must ask ourselves whether or not we have reached our last extremities of what we can bear."

"I will hasten to add," Pendleton said, "that we owe a great deal to Britain, who not only gave us birth, but has protected us with their most superior royal navy."

Pendleton motioned to one of the servants to help him to his feet. Standing behind his chair, both hands resting on its top rail, he continued. "Courage beats within the heart of each person willing to take a stand against the Motherland, whether or not we agree on how to go about it."

"But—" Lee began to rise only to be stopped by Pendleton's raised palm.

"So," Pendleton said, "while most of us agree that Parliament has stepped outside of what she is legally permitted to do, especially with regard to taxes and the need to defend our liberties, we must continue to seek unity as to how to respond. I trust that at next month's meeting of the colonies, we will be able to find that common ground."

Pendleton turned to Peyton Randolph. "I am sure I speak for everyone here when I offer my sincere thanks for the gracious hospitality you have provided for us today."

"Thank you, Colonel Pendleton." Peyton Randolph pushed himself to his feet. "It has been our pleasure, and your thoughts have been most helpful. For those who wish to continue our discussion, shall we adjourn to the parlor?"

As the men scattered, Pendleton made his way around the table. "Mr. Bland, if I can have but a moment of your time."

"Of course." The faltering words tumbled from Bland's lips.

"It was no surprise that the convention elected you, among others, to represent our great colony at the upcoming Congress." Pendleton lowered his voice to a whisper. "It is not an easy trip, and with your health . . ."

Bland's eyes crinkled with a smile. "Never you mind. I have served Virginia for more than three decades and will continue to serve her still."

"If you need anything . . ."

"Thank you." Bland patted Pendleton's forearm.

Pendleton helped his friend to his feet. "Colonel Washington asked me to journey with him to Philadelphia. We have agreed to meet up at Mount Vernon later this month before setting out. Lord willing, I will see you in Congress next month."

Mount Vernon had provided Pendleton with a good night's sleep, and the time had come for him to turn his attention to the journey north. The Potomac River meandered around the plantation, but the lack of breeze it provided on this last day of August mocked its beauty.

"Today looks to be even hotter than yesterday," Pendleton said to Henry and their host, all standing on the back side of Washington's two-and-a-half story home.

Henry kicked at a clot of dirt beneath his feet. "Perhaps we should have left at daybreak."

"My apologies that the piazza isn't yet complete," Washington said. "Not that it would have kept the morning sun at bay, but Mrs. Washington and I hope to use it for afternoon tea. At least on days when the mighty Potomac will cooperate. When it won't, we will let the new cupola work its wonders inside. As for the sweltering ride that lies ahead—"

Henry jumped in. "I look forward to continuing the conversations we began before Colonel Mason and Mr. Triplet departed."

"The servants should have our mounts ready soon," Washington said. "We will get in several hours of riding before the sun goes down. I invited Mr. Lee to journey with us but believe he decided to travel by water and meet us in Philadelphia, along with the others." A frown etched into the side of his mouth. "Let's walk around to the front of the house and see if the shade will provide any relief."

"As much as you entertain, I'm sure the two wings will be a welcome addition," Pendleton said as the men scooted around the north side of the sandstone building, avoiding the end with construction already underway. "Mrs. Washington certainly seems to be in good spirits, even though she speaks to you as a Spartan mother would to her son going off to battle."

Washington wiped his brow. "She tends to keep any anxious thoughts to herself."

The turn around the corner of the house revealed their three body servants adding the finishing touches to the horses.

"Billy," Washington said, "would you please let Mrs. Washington know we are ready to depart."

The manservant dipped his chin, then disappeared into the home.

The three men mounted their horses. The journey of a lifetime was about to begin.

CHAPTER 4

The Journey North

SEPTEMBER 1 - 4, 1774

At the rooster's first call, Patrick Henry had risen to explore the tavern grounds, and the half hour or so of rambling had provided an opportunity to shake off the night's sleep. He squinted against the rising sun threatening to burn off the dew glistening from each blade of grass. His traveling companions would soon pull him back to the dusty roads, and the southerly wind gave promise to another sweltering day.

Strolling past the tavern, he caught a glimpse of his reflection in the window. He hadn't been able to wipe the grin off his face since the association had selected him as one of Virginia's delegates to the General Congress. How would the Lord use him and others whom he had chosen for this task?

Noises from within the stable drew Henry to it, and at his tug, the door creaked open. Inside, the scent of fresh hay tickled his nose. Most of the activity seemed to be coming from the direction of the stalls.

Henry strode over and patted the horse's rump. At the sight of his manservant, he gave a nod. "Good morrow, Pedro. It appears you have us about ready to go."

The black man nodded and swung the saddle onto Henry's horse.

"I trust you slept well," Henry said, "and that all is well in your world."

"The sun's a risin'," the man said as he went about his work, "so I ain't complainin'."

"If anyone has something to complain about 'tis you." Henry shuffled his feet. "Pedro, I cannot deny the inconvenience of living without you—I am ashamed to say it is the very thing that draws me along—but neither can I justify it." Henry put one hand on his hip, then balled up the other and gave it a light shake. "But this trip is about throwing off the chains that bind us. You will see for yourself when we arrive in the big city."

The servant secured the billets to the saddle pad. "Yass, suh."

Henry grabbed the man's forearm, shocking the man to attention.

"You don't understand." Henry stared deep into the man's soul as he released his grasp. "It's about freedom for all. You, me, and all the others who crave it. Hanover County has even spoken out against the African slave trade, and Virginia followed its lead. They wish to see it discouraged altogether. The recent nonimportation agreement even bans the purchase of slaves."

The morning sun glistened off the man's chocolate-brown eyes, stirred at the mention of hope. He jerked his head away from Henry and returned to the task at hand.

"Mr. Henry." Washington's voice came from just inside the building's entrance. "Colonel Pendleton and I have looked everywhere for you."

Henry spun around. "Good day, gentlemen."

"If it is agreeable with you," Washington said, "there is a place a few miles northeast of here where we can stop to breakfast."

Henry patted his belly. "Then let's be on our way."

Pendleton extended one hand toward the entrance and made room for the others to exit. "The innkeeper said when we come upon a tobacco warehouse and half a dozen houses, we will have arrived at the correct hamlet. Beyond that, he believes we could make it to a ferry house by nightfall."

With a slight shake of his head, Henry strode toward his traveling companions. Could the three men be more different? They would be a true representation of their colony at the General Congress. Thus far, various views had made for stimulating conversation and, with three or four more days of travel, additional opportunities were sure to come.

The new day's northeasterly wind brushed Henry's face. A refreshing break from the heat. Rocking in the saddle and the splashing mud against his horse and boots found their rhythm. Evening rains gave way to morning clouds, which had accompanied the three horsemen for hours. Fog hovering over the Delaware River and snaking around the cargo ships sailing up and down her had dissipated. Henry rubbed his neck. A few days of riding had taken their toll, yet the City of Brotherly Love was finally within reach. So much to talk about, yet so little time. Issues they carried with them from Virginia demanded attention, and the dam refused to hold back Henry's desire to discuss them. Washington and the accompanying servants rode in silence amid Henry's conversation with Pendleton, which turned to how the burgesses' inaction regarding court fees impacted their chosen profession.

"But the law that sets court fees had expired," Henry said.

Pendleton took in a deep breath before giving a reply. "Mr. Henry, our job as attorneys is to serve the people. Yet it is more than a job, it is a calling."

"But the fee was no more than a cleverly disguised tax. Taxation without representation."

Pendleton shook his head. "How can a reward to be paid by one man for the services of another be considered a tax, particularly when the reward is a reasonable one? Besides, fees or lack thereof should not be the primary consideration. Fee or no fee, courts are obligated to fulfill their duties by administering justice for the sake of their people."

"Yes, but—"

Pendleton raised a hand. "I will remind you that the convention has spoken and, as much as it may grieve me to leave my dear Caroline County in a state of judicial uncertainty, I have submitted to their decision."

Words sought to tumble from Henry's mouth, but the seniority of the gentleman with whom he spoke restrained him.

"The current circumstances require a united front," Pendleton continued. "But during more normal times, the stopping of the courts should take place under one circumstance alone. Invasion." Pendleton pinched the bridge of his nose before tilting his face in Henry's direction. "And, dear sir, my hope is that it will never take place here."

Washington tugged back on his reins. "Gentlemen, despite the relief of today's weather, I believe both we and our horses could use a short rest."

"Good timing, Colonel." Pendleton said. "This grove of trees will do nicely."

The men dismounted, and turned the horses over to their servants for care. Pendleton retrieved a small blanket from his saddle and spread it under one of the birch trees before having a seat. Then he leaned back against the trunk and closed his eyes. Washington, already standing tall, stretched his arms skyward.

Henry slid down under an oak tree, heaved out a long sigh, then laid back against the cool grass. Light and dark patterns mingled in the clouds above.

Nero, Pendleton's twenty-something body servant, walked over to Henry and held out a ham loaf. "Mista Pendleton said to offer you some."

Henry rolled upward to a cross-legged position and raised his palms to accept the gift. "Thank you, Nero." Henry bit into the savory snack, chewed for a moment, then gulped it down. "Colonel Washington?"

Washington drew in his outstretched arms. "Yes?"

"How did your county fare amid the courts closing?"

"Without the legal authority of the courts, those of us who could step in to fill the void did so." Washington turned his gaze to the horizon.

"Your speech to the association, er, the convention, was impressive. Do you really think you would be able to raise a thousand men and march them to Boston?" Henry took another bite from the ham loaf.

"For their relief," Washington said, turning to face Henry, "and if called upon, I would indeed." Washington reset his focus on the horizon.

Pendleton stirred a bit, but did not open his eyes. "There will be no need for that, gentlemen. Boston has called for us to join them in halting trade with the Motherland, and no more." He opened his eyes but remained motionless. "Our mission is redress, not war. We already have one war too many. Lord Dunmore had no right to declare war on the Shawnees along our colony's western frontier."

Henry chuckled. "No right? 'Twas Indian aggression that started it —the murder of a white man."

Pendleton rolled to his knees, then used the tree trunk to help himself up. "As for those of you who cast a longing eye for the fine lands north of the Ohio and west of the Allegheny Mountain Range . . ." He conveyed a good-natured smile.

Washington moved toward his horse. "I believe our respite has come to an end. We must move on if wish to arrive in time to dine at the new tavern I have heard so much about." He unlatched his saddle bag. "I've been watching the northern sky. You may want to get ready for rain."

Henry groaned, then jumped to his feet to prepare for inclement weather.

"May I suggest," Pendleton said as the three men mounted their horses, "that, on this final leg of our journey, we allow time for reflection. I, for one, need time to collect my wits before our arrival in the big city."

Henry nodded, and the men urged their horses northward, leaving him to collect his thoughts.

Henry squinted against the misting rain, yet the corners of his mouth turned upward. His fingers weaved in and out of the soaked mane of his horse as it carried the rider along. The silence had allowed Henry time to harness recent events that tumbled around in his head, and his heart raced within him.

Songs of liberty, patriotic sermons, and spirited rallies held at Virginia's county courthouses during the summer months had converged to form an inspiring symphony. Despite ambiguities contained in the instructions Virginia had given to its delegates prior to their departure, and their reiterating allegiance to the king, the winds of public opinion were at his back.

"Philadelphia is just around the next bend." Washington's words barely registered as Henry's reflections raced on.

Visiting with George Mason at Mount Vernon just before the three travelers headed north had sent Henry's spirit soaring. Should Henry dare to believe Colonel Mason's flattery? Had Henry really been the most powerful speaker he had ever heard? Were a listener's passions really no longer his own when Henry addressed them? Henry gripped the front edge of his saddle as the three men rounded the bend. Would opportunities arise in Philadelphia for him to harness the sentiments of the delegates who would be gathered there?

The city came into view, and Henry caught his breath. Several church steeples reached to the sky, Philadelphia stretching out beneath them. The largest city in the American colonies was a sight to behold.

As each horseman urged his horse into a canter, Henry mouthed Martha Washington's parting words to them. "I hope you will stand firm," she had said to Pendleton and Henry. "I know George will."

CHAPTER 5

An American?

September 5 - 6, 1774

The stillness of the meeting room settled on Pendleton like a warm blanket on a cold winter's day. A breeze trickled in from the two windows on the northeast corner of the building and teased that the summer heat would soon give way to autumn. Pendleton, senses awakened from a stroll around the room and quick jaunt outside during the break, settled back into the Windsor chair. Ah, comfort for his travel-worn body. Polite nods to several of the forty or so other delegates during his brief excursion, each dressed in his finest attire, seemed to be enough to pacify. For now, he needed some mental solitude amid all the chatter.

He, Henry, and Washington had arrived in Philadelphia amid a light drizzle, but just in time for opening day—the commencement of Congress, as the group decided to refer to themselves. Pendleton, thighs aching from the long journey, resisted the urge to give them a good massage. 'Twas not the time nor the place for such things. If only there had been an additional night's sleep before the start of official meetings, perhaps his anatomy would not be complaining so much.

Pendleton drew in a lungful of air. The faint scent of plaster and sawdust confirmed the newness of the building. He glanced over as his fellow Virginia delegates also returned to their spots in the large semicircle containing the other delegates. With one Virgina delegate yet to arrive, the other three with whom the trio had reconnected upon their arrival soothed his soul in an otherwise foreign land. Muted chatter, a familiar sound in an opening assembly, echoed throughout the twenty-by-thirty-foot room of the cross-shaped building. An empty fireplace graced the long east wall, while a dull light cast a silver glow on the room's activities.

The short walk past the puddles from City Tavern had allowed Pendleton an opportunity to stretch his legs, while whispers around him aroused his suspicions. Had deals been made along the cobblestone street even before the group entered the building? In the end, Pendleton and his conservative colleagues, primarily representing Pennsylvania and New York, had lost the battle to use Pennsylvania's State House for their meetings. Convening in a building held by the Crown might hamper the direction the radicals wanted to take the debate, so the east room of the more neutral Carpenters' Hall would house their deliberations. The curving stairs beckoned Pendleton to explore Benjamin Franklin's new lending library, located above the first-floor gathering space. But it would have to wait.

Pendleton caught the eye of Virginia's own Peyton Randolph—the president, as the group had agreed to call him—now sitting in the semicircle with the other delegates. With Randolph at the helm, Congress was in good hands.

The shuffling of papers drew Pendleton's attention back to the clerk to whom Randolph had given the floor. Pendleton's stomach tightened as the reading of the instructions to each colony's delegates neared. What had they been told? Would they share in Virginia's more conservative approach or were they ready to launch headlong toward independence?

The clerk cleared his throat, then began to read. "'The Province of Massachusetts . . .'"

Pendleton gripped his knee as the clerk read the opening words aloud to the group. What did the most wounded colony believe to be the purpose of this gathering, redress or independence?

"'A meeting of several colonies on this continent is necessary,'" the clerk continued, "'to deliberate and determine upon wise recovery and establishment of their just rights and liberties, civil and religious, and the restoration of union and harmony between Great Britain and the colonies, most ardently desired by all good men.'"

Restoration of union and harmony. Pendleton's heart soared. *Amen and amen.* Surely the remaining colonies had not rushed ahead of those who lived to their north.

"'Samuel Adams, John Adams, and Robert Treat Paine, Esquires,'" the clerk read.

Each man nodded at the mention of his name. The Adams name was familiar enough. Pendleton scrutinized the face of each delegate from Massachusetts Bay as he tied each to his name. If nearly forty years in public service had taught him anything, 'twas the importance of the personal touch when interacting with a colleague.

As the clerk continued, Pendleton hung on every word of the instructions to the delegates from the other colonies, while noting as many names as his fifty-three-year-old brain would allow. His eyes darted around the room. A table and an inkwell for each delegate would have provided an opportunity for recording important facts. Pendleton's attention returned to the clerk.

Rhode Island complained of the taxes placed upon his Majesty's subjects without their consent and of the blocking up of Boston's port. They desired to consult regarding the proper measures needed for obtaining repeal of Parliament's related acts.

Pendleton's body remained motionless while his eyes scanned the faces of other delegates, most stoic and unreadable.

"'From the assembly in Pennsylvania,'" the clerk read.

Another large and important colony.

"'There is an absolute necessity that a congress be held to consult together upon the present unhappy state of the colonies . . .'"

Pendleton breathed a prayer.

"'. . . to form and adopt a plan for the purpose of obtaining redress of American grievances . . .'"

Thank you, Jesus.

"'. . . and for establishing that union and harmony between Great Britain and the colonies, which is indispensably necessary to the welfare and happiness of both.'"

A faint smile tugged at Pendleton's lips as instructions from Delaware and Maryland were read, then from his own colony. He could hold his head high at the pronouncement of Virginia's desires: to obtain redress for Massachusetts Bay, to deal with arbitrary taxes, and to return to harmony with the Motherland. Tension flowed out of Pendleton as every muscle in his body relaxed. The delegates had come together for a united purpose: redress and reconciliation with Great Britain. A return to peace and harmony, not rushing recklessly toward revolution.

Pendleton cast a sideways glance at Henry.

In his mind's eye, Pendleton scanned the list of the thirteen colonies then compared it with the men seated around him. Only eleven colonies represented. Rumors claimed Georgia did not plan to send anyone, but what of North Carolina, John Penn's new home?

A rustling from the New York delegation pulled Pendleton back. One of them stood and faced the rest. "I would like to move that a committee be formed for the purpose of preparing regulations by which this assembly will abide."

All eyes turned to the president, but a stirring from the Massachusetts Bay delegation diverted their attention.

"What sort of regulations?" John Adams had become known to the others when he, in court, defended the soldiers accused of slaughtering five innocent lives in the streets of Boston four and a half years before. "Will we not simply abide by those utilized in England?"

Mumbles. Head nods. Looks of confusion.

"Regulations such as the mode of voting," the man from New York said. "With so much at stake, we should consider the various options. Should each colony cast but one vote or shall those much larger in size carry more weight?"

Silence permeated the room, and no one moved. The morning's differences of opinion over the venue paled in comparison with this topic. It threatened the unity of the group at its very core. And on the first day.

The heart pine floorboards near Pendleton vibrated as Henry pushed his chair back and stood. The hairs on Pendleton's arm stood at attention. *Mr. Henry, please sit down.* Henry's plain gray suit and un-powdered wig would, no doubt, mislead those whom he was about to address. Henry's appearance naturally distorted his youthful thirty-eight years, and his chosen garb gave the impression that the men were about to hear from a country parson, rather than from a Son of Thunder. Then he noticed it—Henry's spectacles pushed to the top of his head. A signal to his audience to prepare for something dramatic.

Henry took two steps forward, then turned to face the majority of those seated before him. "Gentlemen, as the first congress of this sort which has met upon these shores, with the expectation of more, we should exercise wisdom and determine now, rather than later, how these matters will be handled. The practice of the Stamp Act Congress should not set a precedent for our current gathering."

Pendleton's eyes widened. Had Henry's mentioning the Stamp Act Congress from a decade before been a mistake? With its ties to Henry's unbridled attack on Parliament's authority, it had created more than a few adversaries for the then-new burgess. Yet over the years, Henry had mastered his craft and, today, had begun his address without a tinge of strife. Pendleton had seen it time and time again. Henry would wait until they took the bait before reeling them in.

"As you know, that Congress provided but one vote per colony." Henry's tone deepened. "Do you not think it would be a great injustice if a little colony should have the same weight as a greater one?"

Pendleton scanned the room. Several men shifted in their seats.

Careful, Mr. Henry. Choose your words wisely.

A gentleman from New Hampshire spoke. "A little colony has as much at stake as a great one."

Henry bowed his head and extended an arm toward his colleagues. A decade of wrangling with Henry in Virginia's House of Burgesses had provided Pendleton with the ability to speculate as to his intentions. Resolve for the path Henry had started down bubbled beneath his outward performance. Pendleton leaned forward in his chair. *Diplomacy, please.*

Henry continued. "We have gathered during a time of great difficulty and distress. Our circumstances are not unlike a man who calls upon the wisdom of his friends during times of deep trouble. Once something better has been proposed"—he nodded at the delegate from New York—"is it not wise to reject old ways of doing things? Might I suggest that a committee would be able to determine how best to provide each colony with the weight it deserves?"

A gentleman seated near the edge of the semicircle looked at the other delegates and pointed to Henry's back. "Who is he?" he mouthed. Several gave a slight shake of the head while the Virginia delegation remained silent.

Despite their differences, Pendleton could count on the musical quality of Henry's tone to tug at heartstrings while avoiding, or perhaps simply misrepresenting, the details. No one questioned Virginia's status as the most populous colony, yet Henry gave no mention of it, nor that it was the colony he was there to represent.

President Randolph rose from his place in the front of the room. "I believe the delegate from Virginia, Mr. Patrick Henry, has aroused questions in all of us, yet I think it prudent for us to leave the matter until tomorrow."

Pendleton let a slight smile spread to his lips. Randolph would not allow Henry to bring every other delegate to his side, not without serious thought. The wisdom Randolph had obtained as Virginia's leader gave Pendleton comfort. With such a wide array of British colonies represented, additional snares would arise, maybe even other firebrands, yet Randolph's skillful hands would be there to guide Congress in the days that lie ahead.

"It has been a long first day for all of us," Randolph said, "and matters such as these can best be left to simmer before reaching a decision. I will look forward to seeing you here at ten o'clock tomorrow morning. Good day, gentlemen."

Henry arrived early at Carpenters' Hall, ready for any opportunities to convince other delegates that his stand the previous day was worthy of their consideration. Sunbeams filtering through the windows pushed out the dreariness from the day before. A good omen to be sure.

The meeting called to order, fraternizing with his colleagues ceased and Henry took a seat in the semicircle along with the other gentlemen. Henry's knee bounced. How long until they could continue the previous day's debate?

Randolph moved through the preliminaries with grace and speed. "Gentlemen, I believe that takes care of the introductory matters. We are ready to proceed with the heart of what has brought us together. The floor is open for discussion."

It took every fiber of Henry's being to suppress the urge to leap to his feet. Calm and dignity would serve him better today. With the opportunity, he rose slowly and turned to face the delegates. After a few opening remarks, Henry launched into the crux of the matter. All eyes were upon him, and he had no intention of disappointing.

"Need I remind you," he began, "of the treatment Massachusetts Bay has received from Parliament these many years—refusing them the right to assemble, sending troops to lodge among them during times of peace, and finally closing her port to trade?" He meandered to the front of the room where he could get a better view of the delegates, then adapt accordingly. "Such conduct against our sister colony should leave no doubt in your minds that government is dissolved. Our Motherland has forfeited her right to rule us by her own actions." Henry paused, allowing a moment for his words to sink in. "Do not their fleets and armies among us confirm this?"

Henry swept his hand outward and toward the gentlemen now coming under his spell. "Should not the voice of *every* person we represent count in matters that are of concern to them? Where are your boundaries? That part of North America which was once Massachusetts Bay and that part which was once Virginia ought to be considered as having a weight. Will not people complain if ten thousand Virginians have not outweighed one thousand others? The distinctions between Virginians, Pennsylvanians, New Yorkers, and New Englanders are no more." He lifted one hand heavenward, his voice reaching a crescendo. "I am not a Virginian, but an American."

Several gasped.

Henry nodded to his fellow delegates, providing the most gentle and accommodating smile he could muster.

One of Henry's colleagues from the Virginia delegation stirred. "Indeed. If such disrespect should be put upon my fellow countrymen by lessening my colony's vote, I am apprehensive we may never see them at another convention."

Richard Henry Lee, the newly-arrived delegate from Virginia, cleared his throat. "But, Mr. Henry, although your suggestion is most worthy of consideration, would it not be beyond our current abilities to obtain an authentic estimate of how much weight should be given to each colony?"

Henry pushed on. "If we must rely on officers of the Crown to provide authentic accounts, that government is no longer valid and is, therefore, at an end. And we as former subjects should look upon ourselves as one, not as separate colonies."

A delegate from New York rose from his chair. "To the virtue, spirit, and abilities of Virginia we owe much. I should always, therefore, from inclinations as well as justice, be for giving Virginia its full weight."

Henry gave a single nod.

"Should I suppose," the delegate from New York continued, "that we have come here to frame an American constitution, as your proposal would imply, instead of endeavoring to correct the faults in an old one? Instructions we heard yesterday from those we are here to represent declare otherwise. The arbitrary power which concerns us is not yet full, so we must not hasten to actions not yet warranted."

The faces surrounding Henry echoed varying degrees of concern. For many he had crossed the line, and he must quickly mend the fences. He lifted both of his palms toward the group. "If I am overruled, I will humbly submit."

Randolph arose from the leader's chair. "I believe we have heard enough in order to make a decision. Since it is impractical for us to obtain the accurate weight of each colony, we will allow each colony but one vote. Thus," Randolph nodded to the secretary, "we shall resolve to allow one vote per colony until such time we are able to ascertain the importance of each colony."

Henry returned to his chair. He would live to fight another day.

CHAPTER 6

Bloodshed in Boston
SEPTEMBER 6 – OCTOBER 23, 1774

Pendleton nodded at Henry as Virginia's orator took his seat among the other delegates. Congress should indeed form a committee to determine the weight of each colony's vote. Yet, once again, Henry's reasoning and methods differed greatly from Pendleton's. Neither government nor colonial boundaries had disappeared, despite Henry declaring it. Had his bold approach once again caused his defeat? Pendleton shifted in his chair. Four hours of sitting in Carpenters' Hall had taken its toll. If only—

A clamor rose from the direction of the building's entrance. Everyone turned to see a young man burst through the door, hair disheveled and eyes as wide as tea saucers. He bent over, panting. Pendleton's eyes darted to Randolph, whose jaw hung open.

The messenger straightened himself, hands on his hips as he heaved a chestful of air into his adolescent body. "It's Boston. There's been bloodshed."

Several delegates shot to their feet. Others exchanged troubled glances.

"Six killed," the visitor said.

Voices of concern resounded throughout the room. Pendleton sat in stillness, his eyes pinned on the messenger, listening for any news he might bring.

"What?"

"It's happening."

"Are you sure?"

President Randolph motioned for order. "Please come forward, lad."

The young man did as he was told.

"Tell us what you know, from the beginning," Randolph said.

The stranger turned to face the group. "General Gage attempted to seize the people's gunpowder they had stored in Cambridge, near Boston. Thousands, from as far away as Connecticut, took up arms."

"I see," Randolph said. "Then what happened?"

"The British navy that's been sitting in Boston's harbor for months shelled the town."

Pendleton clenched his fingers, ignoring his pounding heart as he took in the scene. Cries of "War! War!" from townsfolk penetrated the building's walls.

"Six of the townsfolk were killed."

President Randolph took a step forward. "Gentlemen, this obviously demands our attention. However, before we open the floor for discussion, we must first obtain a clearer picture. I propose that we scatter about town to collect any tidbits of information we can. We will reconvene here at five o'clock."

Many nodded, then dispersed.

Pendleton sat in silence, a warmth of emotion flowing into his cheeks.

The shedding of blood threatened to change everything. Faces of the young men he knew and loved raced through his mind—neighbors, friends, and family. Their lives must not be disturbed with the cruelties of war, nor their families forced to accept its bitter pill. The harsh taste of his own losses from decades gone by lingered with him still. Experience had taught him the pain of living without a father, a pain he wanted no one else to bear. Britain's actions would make it more difficult, but he must find a way to prevent the matter from escalating further. Surely bloodshed would give everyone reason to pause and seek alternative means toward resolution.

A tap on his shoulder pulled him back to his surroundings. He locked eyes with his colleague, Mr. Lee, then accompanied him into town to learn more.

Church bells tolled the sound of death.

Pendleton eased into the Windsor chair to which he had grown accustomed. The morning walk to Carpenters' Hall had left him a bit unsettled. Townsfolk running here and there with hints of revenge upon their lips placed the city in a state of utter confusion. Much had changed since the meetings from the day before. The now-darkened room which greeted the delegates to Carpenters' Hall provided a refuge. Curtains, pulled tight around the windows, and the locked door kept any secrets inside the walls. Flickering candles from the chandelier cast eerie shadows across the faces of the delegates. Muffled sounds of tolling bells and continued cries of war filtered through. Pendleton's pocket watch showed nine o'clock, the time the delegates had agreed for opening each session with prayer. Matters of business would begin at ten.

Henry, seated at the other end of the Virginia table, fiddled with the knife-shaped paper cutter that he carried with him. Pendleton suppressed a smile. Perhaps the new rules of order were the result of Henry's less-than-restrained speeches. No person should speak more than twice on the same point, unless allowed by the majority, and no issues that arose should be settled on the same day.

The Anglican clergyman stepped to the front of the room and met Pendleton's smile with one of his own. Despite the many religious sects among them—Quakers, Anabaptists, and Presbyterians—Samuel Adams had wisely suggested that someone of a persuasion with close ties to the Church of England present the morning prayer. Seeing a minister from the long-established church brought peace to Pendleton's soul.

Reverend Jacob Duché's white wig and robe provided the sense that the Lord's presence hovered near. His gentle, yet serious, eyes scanned the men seated before him. "Gentlemen, I believe Providence has not forgotten us. On this day, he has led me to a passage from the Holy Scriptures which is as alive today as it was on the day King David penned it." The reverend opened his prayer book, then placed a pair of eyeglasses on his nose. "I will be reading from the thirty-fifth Psalm."

A hush settled over the room as the minister began to read.

"'Plead my cause, O Lord, with them that strive with me: fight against them that fight against me. Take hold of shield and buckler. Draw out also the spear, and stop the way against them that persecute me: say unto my soul, I am thy salvation.'"

Pendleton shifted in his chair. *Fight . . . shield . . . spear.*

No, Lord. Not that. But yes, you are our salvation.

The clergyman's eyebrows perched low as the words fell from his lips. "'Let them be confounded and put to shame that seek after my soul.'"

Lord, please teach our Motherland the error of her ways.

"'For without cause have they hid for me their net in a pit.'"

Lord, please protect us all from harm, even those who have been led astray.

"'False witnesses did rise up. They rewarded me evil for good.'" The minister adjusted his spectacles. "'But as for me, when they were sick, I behaved myself as though he had been my friend or brother.'"

Yes, Lord, help us to treat Britain as our friend, not as an enemy.

"'Let not them that are mine enemies wink with the eye that hate me without a cause. For they speak not peace.'"

Pendleton dared to examine the faces of those around him. Most pinned their gazes on the minister, while others stared at the floor or elsewhere, as if to sear every word upon their hearts.

"'This thou hast seen, O Lord: keep not silence.'"

You be the one to plead our case. Turn Britain's adversarial heart toward peace.

"'Judge me, O Lord my God, according to thy righteousness. Let them be ashamed and brought to confusion together that rejoice at mine hurt.

"'Let them shout for joy, and be glad, that favor my righteous cause. And my tongue shall speak of thy righteousness and of thy praise all the day long.'"

Reverend Duché raised his head from the reading. "The Word of the Lord." He closed the prayer book and lifted his hands upward. "Let us pray."

Several gentlemen stood, turned, and knelt by their chairs. Pendleton's eyes welled up with tears as he did the same, despite the objection of his aging knees.

A moment of silence passed before the clergyman raised his voice to heaven. "O Lord our heavenly Father, high and mighty King of kings, and Lord of lords, who dost from thy throne behold all the dwellers on earth and reignest with power supreme and uncontrolled over all the kingdoms, empires, and governments—"

Several "Amens" arose from around the room.

"Look down in mercy on these our American colonies, who have fled to thee from the rod of the oppressor and thrown themselves on thy gracious protection, desiring to be henceforth dependent only on thee."

"Yes, Lord," Pendleton whispered.

"To thee have they appealed for the righteousness of their cause. Take them, therefore, heavenly Father, under thy nurturing care. Give them wisdom in council and valor in the field. Defeat the malicious designs of our cruel adversaries." The minister's voice rose. "Convince them of the unrighteousness of their cause and constrain them to drop the weapons of war from their unnerved hands in the day of battle."

"Let it be, dear Lord," cried one of the delegates.

The reverend let out a stifled groan. "Be thou present, O God of wisdom, and direct the councils of this honorable assembly. Enable them to settle things on the best and surest foundation that the scene of blood may be speedily closed so that order, harmony, and peace may be effectually restored amongst the people."

Pendleton's torso swayed in agreement. *Please, God.*

"Preserve the health of their bodies and vigor of their minds. Shower down on them and the millions they here represent, such temporal blessings as thou seest expedient, and crown them with everlasting glory in the world to come. All this we ask in the name and through the merits of Jesus Christ, thy Son and our Savior. Amen."

A flood of thanksgiving poured through Pendleton's body, still kneeling by his chair. He lifted his lids and pulled out his handkerchief to wipe his eyes.

A nearby gentleman offered a hand up, whispering, "Worth riding one hundred miles to hear."

Pendleton's knees wobbled as he found his seat. Around him, tears flowed freely, even among the Pennsylvania Quakers.

No one wanted to break the spell.

Henry's heart did a jig as he ascended the stairs to City Tavern, the unofficial meeting place for the delegates outside of Carpenters' Hall. The tavern had become a hub of news, activity, and gossip. With nearly two weeks of meetings behind them, Henry had sorted out many of the names and faces of his colleagues. Yet, amid all the large-group chatter and challenging schedule, time with each one was more difficult to come by.

He stepped into the entrance hall and drew in the scent of all things scrumptious. As a major port, Philadelphia boasted of dishes from around the world. Caribbean pepperpot stew had already become a favorite. Lately, the hint of certain spices would carry him home. *Home.* Leaving Sarah in the care of others . . . . He shook his head. Surely she would be fine. The flurry of activity in the large room pulled his mind back to his surroundings.

Large windows and benches nestled around the various hearths provided a genteel reception. Less than a year old, the tavern boasted of five floors, three dining rooms, two coffee rooms, five lodging rooms, and an enormous ballroom. A perfect place to mingle with the other delegates both before and after official gatherings. Today, he had accepted an invitation from someone he had only known through newspapers during the Boston Massacre trials. With hundreds of miles between their respective homes, it took a congress of all the colonies to bring the two men together.

A middle-aged hostess suddenly appeared in one of the doorways, tucking away a roaming strand of hair. "Mr. Henry?"

Henry gave a clipped nod.

"Your dinner partner has already arrived. This way, please."

The hostess guided Henry through the maze of tables, chairs, and the buzz of conversations already underway, stopping at a table for two under a large window. She extended her hand to the available chair. The formal attire of the man awaiting Henry's arrival emitted an aristocratic air.

"Thank you." Henry claimed his seat.

"We will be with you shortly," the hostess said before scurrying away to tend to other guests.

"Mr. Henry," John Adams said, "what a pleasure."

Henry sat back in his chair, delighted with the aura of the people and place. "The pleasure is mine, I assure you."

After placing their orders, the conversation began to flow beyond the niceties.

With his applewood smoked pork chop and sweet potato biscuits half eaten, Henry launched in. "So, why would *you* want to meet *me*?"

John Adams fingered his mug. "Any Virginian who would dare to take a stand during the Stamp Act crisis while surrounded by his more traditional colleagues, especially a decade ago, is someone I want to meet. To be truthful, it took me longer to come aboard than it did you."

"Some would say it was due to my inexperience." Henry's stomach bounced with laughter. "I gave that speech mere days after taking my seat as a burgess."

Adams's eyebrow lifted. "Would you do it now?"

"Without question. Tyranny, whether through taxation without representation or any other form, must not be allowed to go unchecked."

Adams nodded.

Henry lifted an eyebrow. "I thought news about bloodshed in Boston might have awakened other delegates from their slumber. Perhaps the subsequent information that those rumors were false will mute any such response."

"The more truthful report seemed to be an answer to the prayers from the day before." Adams pushed his plate away and stared deep within Henry. "I'm sorry that many had to endure a couple miserable days of excitement and anxiety before the facts became more clear. If the earlier rumors had proven true, even my dear wife back in Massachusetts Bay would have heard the thunder of an American Congress."

A grin spread across Adams's face. "While British soldiers' taking the colony's gunpowder is of concern, the resolves that Mr. Revere delivered from my colony today, and Congress' response to them, has made this one of the happiest days of my life. This day convinced me that America will support Massachusetts Bay or will perish with her. It lit a fire under the delegates without bloodshed."

"The timing," Henry said, "certainly seemed providential."

Adams pointed up. "My cousin Samuel is attentive to his voice and would not miss an opportunity to help move the delegates in the right direction."

Henry set down his cup. "But Samuel Adams was here, not back in Boston."

"Samuel's premonition skills are well refined. He knows how to set things up in advance so they are brought to light at just the right time."

A fresh energy filled Henry's spirit. "I see." The Adams cousins were proving to be quite a duo.

Adams motioned for someone to come clear the table. He pulled papers from his pocket, which he laid on the table in front of him. "I would like to share a letter with you that I picked up from one of my allies while on my way to Philadelphia. My friend believes that Britain's policies are intolerable. If left unchallenged, our posterity will never live in freedom." Adams motioned to the papers before him. "He says we must fight."

Henry banged his fist on the table. "By God, I am of that man's mind." Other patrons turned toward the disturbance before turning back to their own conversations.

Adams pushed the pages toward Henry. "Would you like to review it for yourself?"

"Indeed." Henry picked up the letter, mouthing its opening words, "'We must fight.'" He scanned further, then read aloud. "'It is now or never that we must assert our liberty.'"

He glanced up and proclaimed, "I love this."

Adams pushed himself to his feet. "I will leave you to enjoy it while I speak briefly with a gentleman across the room."

Henry nodded and went back to reading.

A few minutes later, Adams returned to his seat. "Your thoughts?"

Henry tapped his index finger on the papers. "I agree with this writer. We must make plans for military actions, whether or not we declare it publicly."

"I cannot agree with everything he says, but I must say that I am impressed with both the candor and courage with which you acknowledge your views." Adams scanned the room before turning back to Henry. "There is no guarantee, but I will speak with some others, including my cousin, to see if we might be able to get you added to the Grand Committee. Defining our rights is turning out to be more challenging than we could have imagined. By now, others may see the fairness in giving the larger colonies a greater voice."

"Thank you." Henry said, a fresh energy welling up within. "Thank you, indeed."

The morning fog hid the nearby stable and the glorious colors of the late October day as Pendleton stroked his horse's mane. "Well, ol' boy, the time has finally come to head home. Two months of meetings have worn me to the bone."

Pendleton turned his head to cough.

"Colonel Pendleton." The voice came from behind him.

Pendleton turned to see one of the Pennsylvania delegates approaching. "Mr. Galloway, what a surprise."

"Are you leaving us?"

"As much as I would like to stay and see it to the end," Pendleton said, struggling to project a sincerity that he in no way felt, "my body is telling me otherwise."

"No one can deny that it has been a grueling couple of months," Joseph Galloway said. The angled eyes of the staunch loyalist made it even more difficult to trust him. "You must be pleased with the decision to include the laws of nature as part of the colonies' argument against the Ministry."

"Yes, I—"

Nero emerged from the fog, accepting the horse's reins from his master. Pendleton shot Nero a quick thank-you with his eyes. With a dozen years behind them, Nero could sense when his master needed help.

Pendleton forced down a cough that threatened to escape, then turned back to Galloway. "Thank you for your attempt to provide a path toward reconciliation. I am sorry the delegates were not more receptive to your ideas."

"I am afraid my efforts pushed the majority in the opposite direction."

"Our official petition to the king says otherwise. For now, we must await his reply." Pendleton tipped his head toward Nero. "I apologize, Mr. Galloway, but my traveling party awaits."

"I hope to see you back here in the spring when we reconvene. In the meantime, I wish you a good trip back to Virginia." Galloway nodded a goodbye before disappearing into the fog.

The cough Pendleton had suppressed throughout the exchange broke free. He bent over with one arm against his chest, wheezing and coughing freely, his eyes welling up with tears.

Nero ran to the stable and returned with a blanket, then draped it around Pendleton's shoulders. "We'll get you back to Virginia, Mista Pendleton, and nurse you back to health. You'll see."

CHAPTER 7

𝔚𝔦𝔫𝔡𝔰 𝔬𝔣 𝔠𝔥𝔞𝔫𝔤𝔢

NOVEMBER 1774 – FEBRUARY 1775

The long journey from Philadelphia behind him, Henry had settled once again into his Scotchtown home. Its sights and sounds had become both a blessing and a curse. He cherished time spent with his children and all the conveniences of home, yet the voice of his wife emitting from the bedroom had become almost more than he could bear. "Free me, free me!" she cried, desperate to be released from the body that bound her. Futile attempts to calm her, by him and others of the household, left little room for encouragement. Joy at the birth of their sixth child three years before had quickly turned to confusion and desperation as Sarah's health and state of mind began to decline. The change of scenery brought on by the new home had not brought about the effect for which everyone had hoped.

Henry rose from the chair at his desk and made a straight line for the passageway. "Pedro?"

"Yass, suh." The servant quickly came to his master's side.

"See to it that the Hanover militiamen receive word to meet me at

59

Smith's Tavern. I have something of great importance to communicate to them. I will get the particulars to you by the end of the day."

Henry moved past his body servant and out the door, with calls of "Give me liberty!" from the bedroom following him.

The brisk autumn air would help him collect his thoughts. The colonies must defend their rights, and taking up arms would be the first step.

The Caroline County courthouse fit Pendleton like an old shoe, even more familiar than the military boots he wore while leading his county's militiamen. Today, a mix of seasoned public servants and those for whom the experience was new, nineteen men in all, sat before him as Caroline County's week-old Committee of Safety. One more committee he now chaired. His nephew, namesake, and protegee, Edmund Jr., was among them. Although nearly two months had passed since returning home, repercussions of the Grand Congress meetings were just beginning to materialize. Signing his name to the association document before departing Philadelphia resulted in the scene before him—a local manifestation of what the joint colonies had formed.

Shadows from the crackling fire played with those from days gone by, days when Pendleton could simply assist Major Robinson with anything and everything the court required. But with the passage of time, the mantle had fallen on him. Hardly big enough for today's meeting, a small oak table had been pushed to the middle of the room to accommodate a few of the men. Others pulled in chairs from around the room, placing them hodgepodge behind those seated at the table, while younger men made use of the floor.

"Caroline County has commissioned us," Pendleton began, placing the tips of his fingers on the table in front of him, "to ensure that pledges made by hundreds of Virginia merchants last month are kept. And though two years' worth of English goods lie stored up in our warehouses, already some continue to carry on trade with the Motherland."

Pendleton tilted his head toward the man seated at a nearby desk, scribbling away with a quill. "Our hope is that the confession you heard from Mr. Morris today and apology he now writes for publication will encourage others to honor their pledge. By doing so, they will not need to undergo a similar act of humiliation."

Morris laid down the quill and turned his attention to Pendleton.

"If you have completed the task, you may bring it to me." Pendleton held out his hand.

Morris obliged, and Pendleton motioned for him to remain standing beside him. The two men shifted to shield their eyes from the December sun filtering through one of the windows.

"'I do, therefore, confess my sincere sorrow,'" Pendleton read aloud from the paper he held, "'for not concurring in the association. Hopes that this will prove satisfactory to the gentlemen of this county who had so just a cause of complaint. I confess my error in hopes that my future behavior will be a means of my regaining their esteem.'" He placed a hand on the man's forearm. "Thank you, Mr. Morris. We will see that this is delivered to the *Gazette* for publication. Thank you for your time and cooperation. You are free to go."

The door creaked shut behind the young man as he slipped out, and Pendleton turned to the next item on the agenda.

"Before we begin our discussion regarding ceiling prices of corn, collecting tea, and the inspection of merchants' books, I'd like to remind you to please tell your neighbors that our court is ready and willing to handle any matters that might concern them. In general, we will be open for business on the same days our committee meets."

One of the young men on the floor leaned forward. "I know several in my area who will be much obliged."

Pendleton shuffled back to his chair, then eased into it. He double-tapped one finger on the table to insure the men's attention. "I should also make you aware of a matter of great interest. As a few of you may have heard, Lord Dunmore's victory over the Shawnee along the Ohio River has been tempered by news that Great Britain has announced no more arms or ammunition will be exported to the colonies. This is of grave concern."

A few men nodded while another planted his fist on the table, causing a few to jump. "What?" the man said.

"Surely, some will find a way," one of the men said with a twinkle in his eye, "since many American merchants have experience smuggling items in. Of course, some are caught."

"Governors have been instructed," Pendleton said, "to prevent the landing of such items that make it to our shores. So, they will be more vigilant than ever. We certainly cannot count on supplies flowing freely. I alerted Lieutenant Woodford, and he and I are doing what we can to prepare our county's militia. While seeking peace with the Motherland, we must continue to prepare for the unthinkable."

At times, Pendleton wondered if choosing a north-facing room for his library had been best. With one of the coldest winters in memory, house servants scurried about to attend to the needs of their master and the four young men—three in their twenties plus a fifteen-year-old lad —gathered for another day of learning. Oh, how he enjoyed pouring into their lives. With so many sessions missed in recent months due to travel and other responsibilities, there was much to cover.

Movement from the interior doorway caught Pendleton's eye. A servant stood with an arm filled with logs for the fire. Pendleton gave him a nod and a quick thank-you. Warmth from the hearth to Pendleton's left kept the cold at bay, while curtains at the room's other end struggled to keep out the gusty winds beating against the library's only window. Rolled-up rags sat at the base of the door, preventing the cold from becoming unbearable.

"'Blows must decide,'" Pendleton said, standing at the head of the mammoth table, "'whether the colonies are to be subject to Great Britain or be independent,' are hardly the words of a loving king."

One of the young men seated around the table stirred. "If the king wants to come down on us with the first blow, then we will fight back."

The others uttered sounds of affirmation.

"Many are ready and willing to fight," Pendleton said, "but that doesn't mean that we should. Not until every other option has been exhausted." He turned and stared into the flames. "The cost of war is high. A few months ago, at least seventy died in the Ohio Country. Multiply that many times over if we decide to take on the most powerful force in the world."

Pendleton pivoted back to the young men, three with looks of concern, and the lad at the end of the table with jaw locked tight. "Our neighbors are beginning to use the antiquated terms Whig and Tory," Pendleton said. "Those terms emerged in the last century when certain revolutionary principles were being debated."

"I hear there are more Whigs about our streets than Tories."

"You may be right. And we can be thankful. Yet there are still Tories among us."

"But what does it mean?"

Pendleton slid around the table and pulled a book from one of the shelves. "John Locke, who lived about a hundred years ago, and others left us with many things to contemplate regarding the theory of government. Kings exist to serve the people and are neither divine nor invincible. Subjects have the right to push back if a royal abuses the authority given to him. I would not lead our county's militia unless I believed this."

One of the young men slammed his fist on the table. "King George has abused his authority, and we must fight."

The others nodded.

Pendleton lifted a hand. "The Whig tradition allows for the people to raise a militia not only in self-defense, but also as a means to remedy the abuse of power in a constitutional way. Tories are loyal to the king and believe he is right to fight against the threat of American independence."

One of the youths scrunched up his face. "But you are a Whig, yet you don't believe we should fight."

"Fighting is the right thing to do," Pendleton said, "if and when it is the last resort. Many refer to those of us who believe this way, and are seeking redress with the Motherland, as conservatives. Those who move about with 'independence' on their lips and insist the time has already come to do battle, such as Patrick Henry and John Adams, are referred to as radicals."

"So, there are two kinds of Whigs, conservative and radical?"

"Correct. On many matters the Whigs and Tories agree, such as taxation only with our consent, that our rights are in danger, and that we should stand ready with a militia. Many disagree, however, with regards to how and when we should defend those rights."

The lad at the end of the table jumped up. "I think we should go ahead and fight, and be done with it."

Pendleton's shoulders bobbed with his faint chuckle. "Many wish it were that simple."

The lad placed his hands on his hips. "But—"

Pendleton lifted a hand. "With permission from your folks, I will be happy to give you some preliminary lessons in the art of war so when you are old enough to fight . . ."

The lad threw an imaginary musket over his shoulder, then marched a few steps. "Yes, sir, Colonel. I want to be ready to take them on!"

"In the meantime," Pendleton said, "a few weeks from now, Virginia's county representatives will gather once again as a convention to find a path forward." The howling wind rattled the window. "If, that is, the winter gale will subside and not simply blow us out to sea."

CHAPTER 8

Liberty or Death!

MARCH 23, 1775

The winds of late March had shifted, blowing away the warmth of the opening day of Virginia's Convention, three days prior. Pendleton squinted at the clouds, a heartfelt "brr" escaping his lips as he hurried up the stone steps and into the churchyard. Snow was on its way, but concerns for his crops back home would have to wait. He made his way to the meeting amid the townsfolk who milled about. Others had bundled up and perched on the sills of the church's open windows, apparently not willing to get their information secondhand. If only the three days of wins by the conservatives could continue. Yet the resolution he held in his pocket would provide the opportunity for the radicals to push back or to accept a more sensible approach.

Pendleton hastened around to the main entrance located on the building's broad side, then slid past others coming and going. He shook the cold from his body as he stepped inside and surveyed the scene. The main portion of Richmond's parish church, the only building in town large enough to house the convention, swept to his left, about twice as wide as it was deep, with two aisles running the length. The delegates—Jefferson, Washington, and more than a hundred others—had taken their seats inside the pew boxes.

Fifty miles and two days ride by horseback from Williamsburg, the new location was out of the reach of Lord Dunmore, his troops, and the British warships. Delegates mingled with colleagues who had just arrived from the western frontier, now free to travel since the threat from Indians had lessened. If the royal governor believed his role in ending the war with the Indians would make Virginians forget his other reckless behavior, he was sadly mistaken.

Pendleton spotted the man with whom he wanted to have a private moment, yet no opportunity had come. Patrick Henry sat across the room, not far from the enclosed chancel and raised pulpit. Ignoring his own ache within, Pendleton paced off the short distance. Mere words could not wash away certain sorrows, yet he desired to help carry the load. "Mr. Henry?"

Henry raised his bent head.

"Mr. Henry," Pendleton said, "may I have a moment of your time?"

Heartbreak mingled with resolve in Henry's eyes. "Certainly."

"My prayers and sympathies are with you at the loss of your dear wife. If there is anything I can do . . ."

Henry's chin dipped into a nod. "She is now free from the chains which bound her."

The clerk called the meeting to order. Pendleton provided an understanding smile to Henry before moving to the front-row seat left open for him.

During the opening invocation, the reverend addressing their heavenly Father as the only ruler of princes sat well with him. But should they continue to pray that King George would have the strength to overcome all his enemies? Had the prayer become one they now prayed against themselves?

The clerk stood and read the previous day's minutes. Although not without debate, Virginia's Convention had ultimately approved the proceedings and resolutions of the American Continental Congress and thanked the delegates who had represented them there.

With preliminaries behind them, Pendleton requested the floor. He stood and pivoted to face the delegates. "Although it is rather lengthy, Mr. President, I move that the petition from Jamaica's assembly be read in its entirety. Since they too are a British colony, their arguments are a reflection of our own concerns. It is only fair that we have these details clearly in our minds before we begin the debate."

The motion was seconded, and Pendleton returned to his seat.

The clerk shuffled a few papers, then glanced at his audience. "I will read Jamaica's petition to King George III, dated December 1774."

Its contents already familiar, as the *Gazette* had published its sentiments a couple weeks before, Pendleton took a few moments to scan the crowd. He could count on verbal opposition from Richard Henry Lee, but Washington's and Jefferson's resistance would be quieter in nature.

The clerk continued to read, "'. . . that no law can affect them but such as receive their assent, given by themselves or their representatives . . .'"

Pendleton continued to assess the delegates. Nicholas and Nelson would back him.

More of Jamaica's petition interrupted Pendleton's thoughts. "'Colonists shall have the same privileges . . . as the freeborn subjects of England . . . those very rights and privileges which prompted their emigration.'"

And other delegates were as yet undecided, those he would need to convince through the strength of his arguments. Would his words be enough to sway them?

The clerk droned on. "'Your humble petitioners have, for several years, with deep and silent sorrow, lamented this unrestrained exercise of legislative power, still hoping to avert that last and greatest of calamities.'"

The clerk returned to his seat, and President Randolph took his place on the platform at the front of the room.

The president nodded toward Pendleton. "Colonel Edmund Pendleton of Caroline County."

Pendleton stood. "I would like to offer a resolution in response to Jamaica's petition."

All eyes turned to Pendleton as he began to read. "'That the unfeigned thanks and most grateful acknowledgement of this convention be presented to that very respectable assembly for the exceedingly generous and affectionate part they have so nobly taken in the unhappy contest between Great Britain and her colonies. And for their truly patriotic endeavors to fix the just claims of the colonists upon the most permanent constitutional principles. That the assembly be assured it is the most ardent wish of this colony—and we're persuaded of the whole continent of North America—to see a speedy return to those halcyon days when we lived a free and happy people.'"

Pendleton turned back to Randolph. "Thank you, Mr. President," he said, then took his seat.

The treasurer of the colony and ally of Pendleton, Robert C. Nicholas, stood. "Mr. President, I believe Colonel Pendleton has done a most admirable job of thanking those in Jamaica for their patriotism, and I desire to second Colonel Pendleton's resolution and see that it is forwarded to this island of the West Indies." Nicholas sat down.

What a comfort to have others in the room who also understood the importance of thoughtful actions at this critical juncture.

"All in favor," President Randolph said, "let it be known by saying, 'Aye.'"

"Ayes" went up around the room.

"All opposed, 'No.'" The president scanned the crowd.

Silence.

"Then the clerk will forward these resolutions to Jamaica's Speaker at the earliest opportunity."

Henry rose to his feet. "Mr. President, I too, have a resolution."

His tone reflected determination. Pendleton swiveled on his pew to face the one speaking.

President Randolph motioned to Henry. "Mr. Patrick Henry of Hanover County."

"Gentlemen," Henry began, "while the desire to see a return to the halcyon days of old is commendable, those peaceful and harmonious days are no longer within our grasp if we but sit by quietly. We can thank the assembly in Jamaica for its patriotic endeavors, yet we must address the heart of their petition—how we as a people must respond."

Henry unfolded a paper, lifted his chin, then faced his audience. "I, therefore, present the following resolutions:

"'Resolved, that a well-regulated militia is the natural strength and only security of a free government.'"

Audible gasps rippled throughout the room. Pendleton sat motionless, wanting to hear every word before formulating a response.

"'That such a militia in this colony would forever render it unnecessary for the Mother Country to keep among us, for the purpose of our defense, any standing army of mercenary forces, always subversive of the quiet, and dangerous to the liberties of the people, and would obviate the pretext of taxing us for their support.'"

"Remember Boston," someone whispered from across the aisle.

Henry acknowledged the comment with a nod, then resumed reading. "'That the establishment of such a militia is at this time peculiarly necessary, by the state of our laws for the protection and defense of the country, some of which have already expired, and others will shortly do so.'"

Henry squared his shoulders. "'Resolved, therefore, that this colony be immediately put into a posture of defense—'"

Several tapped their walking sticks against the floor in disgust. Every fiber in Pendleton's body stood at attention.

"'And that a committee prepare a plan for the embodying, arming, and disciplining such a number of men as may be sufficient for that purpose.'"

Lee, Henry's ally whose proposal for military defense Henry had seconded in Congress, took to his feet. "Mr. President, we must not wait until Britain has closed our ports to trade, as they have already done in Boston. I second Mr. Henry's resolutions."

Enough. Pendleton grabbed the frame of the pew box and pulled himself to his feet.

"Mr. President," Benjamin Harrison said before Pendleton could speak, "would this not be premature? Mr. Henry himself was present when the Congress agreed to send a petition to his Majesty. Is he, along with the rest of us, not obligated to wait for a reply before suggesting such measures?"

Pendleton stepped out of the pew box and nodded to Mr. Harrison. "Indeed. Mr. Henry's prophecy of war and desire to prepare for battle *is* premature. The monetary battle is the one we must continue to fight, not a battle that results in bloodshed. With the refusal to trade with Great Britain as our ammunition, the Motherland will, in the course of time, see the error of her ways. I do not expect them to en-force Parliament's acts by force, as some would suggest."

Pendleton pivoted to face the others. "When declaring war, as Mr. Henry's resolutions do behind but a thin veil, one should not build a tower without first considering whether or not he has sufficient funds to finish it. Likewise, one should not rush to war without the necessary preparations. Among other things, foreign allies must be gathered to help protect against the impending storm. Those who wish to continue to prepare quietly may do so. But no words of war should be declared publicly until we have heard back from the king. Let us be patient. For as certain as I am standing before you today, blood will follow the armies."

A stir came from the direction of Jefferson, known more for his skillful pen than for his spoken word. Pendleton furrowed his brow. Perhaps Jefferson's opposition would not be as hushed as he had imagined.

Jefferson stood resolute. "I respectfully disagree with my friends and fellow delegates." His treble voice steady, but hushed. "Although the Jamaican petition claims that our rights come from the king rather than from the British constitution and natural law, their severe rebuke to our Motherland is well deserved. And their urging the king to act as a mediator between us and his British subjects is too late. I believe it is time that we fight back, so I desire that we move forward with accepting Mr. Henry's resolutions."

Pendleton's raised hand reclaimed the delegate's attention. "I will remind this body not only of the need to await a reply from his Majesty, but also of how ill-prepared both we and our fellow colonies are. To push forward with Mr. Henry's proposal at this time would ensure defeat. Patience is a virtue given to us for such a time as this. The pledge of nonresistance by Jamaica's assembly, rather than rushing to war, is appropriate. Any gentleman present who has patriotism in his soul, of whom I am chief, must at this time allow that patience to surface. Otherwise, our country will be no more."

The arguments for restraint laid out, Pendleton bowed his head and rested his case.

Pendleton returned to his pew box and sat in silence.

"Mr. President?" Henry's voice rang strong as he rose and looked over those gathered.

The president tilted his head. "Mr. Henry."

A fire burned within Henry's eyes, yet a calmness had settled over the rest of his body. He had postured himself as a minister about to address his congregation on the Sabbath, his spectacles atop his head. Pendleton shifted to keep watch over the reactions. Everyone appeared focused on Henry in expectation.

Henry turned to face the delegates. "No man thinks more highly than I do of the patriotism, as well as abilities, of the very worthy gentlemen who have just addressed the House. But different men often see the same subject in different lights. And therefore, I hope it will not be thought disrespectful to those gentlemen if I shall speak forth my sentiments freely and without reserve.

"This is no time for ceremony. The question before the House is one of awful moment to this country." Henry drew in a breath, then continued. "For my own part, I consider it as nothing less than a question of freedom or slavery, and in proportion to the magnitude of the subject, ought to be the freedom of the debate. It is only in this way that we can hope to arrive at truth and fulfill the great responsibility which we hold to God and our country. Should I keep back my opinions at such a time, through fear of giving offense, I should consider myself as guilty of treason toward my country and of an act of disloyalty toward the Majesty of heaven, which I revere above all earthly kings."

Henry extended his arm toward Randolph while keeping the focus on his audience. "Mr. President, it is natural for man to indulge in the illusions of hope. We are apt to shut our eyes against a painful truth." Henry leaned over and gripped the railing in front of him. "Is this the part of wise men engaged in a great and arduous struggle for liberty?"

He pulled himself upright and shook his head. "For my part, whatever anguish of spirit it may cost, I am willing to know the whole truth."

Pendleton rubbed one hand against his thigh, then gripped his knee. The whole truth, yes. But may reason and wisdom prevail.

"I know of no way of judging the future but by the past. And judging by the past, I wish to know what there has been in the conduct of the British Ministry for the last ten years to justify those hopes with which gentlemen have been pleased to solace themselves. Is it that insidious smile with which our petition has been lately received?" Henry waved a finger in the air. "Trust it not, sir. It will prove a snare to your feet. Suffer not yourselves to be betrayed with a kiss.

"Are fleets and armies necessary to a work of love and reconciliation? Let us not deceive ourselves. I ask, gentlemen, what means this martial array, if its purpose be not to force us to submission?"

Pendleton pulled at his collar.

"And what have we to oppose to them? Shall we try argument? We have been trying that for the last ten years. What terms shall we find which have not been already exhausted? We have done everything that could be done to avert the storm which is now coming on. We have petitioned. We have remonstrated. We have supplicated. We have prostrated ourselves before the throne and have implored its interposition to arrest the tyrannical hands of the Ministry and Parliament. Our petitions have been slighted. Our remonstrances have produced additional violence and insult. Our supplications have been disregarded, and we have been spurned with contempt from the foot of the throne. In vain, after these things, may we indulge the fond hope of peace and reconciliation?"

The muscles in Henry's face tightened. "There is no longer any room for hope. If we wish to be free, we must fight. I repeat it, sir, we must fight! An appeal to arms and to the God of hosts is all that is left us."

"Treason!" several shouted at the suggested violence. Others sat with eyes wide or mouths hung open.

Henry motioned for silence. "They tell us that we are weak, unable to cope with so formidable an adversary." Henry fixed his pleading eyes upon Pendleton as his tone intensified. "But when shall we be stronger? Will it be when we are totally disarmed and when a British guard shall be stationed in every house? Shall we gather strength by inaction? Shall we acquire the means of effectual resistance by lying supinely on our backs and hugging the delusive phantom of hope, until our enemies shall have bound us hand and foot?" Henry flung open the door to his pew box and stepped out.

"Sir, we are not weak if we make a proper use of those means which the God of nature hath placed in our power. The millions of people, armed in the holy cause of liberty, and in such a country as that which we possess, are invincible by any force which our enemy can send against us. Besides, sir, we shall not fight our battles alone. There is a just God who presides over the destinies of nations, and who will raise up friends to fight our battles for us."

Pendleton glanced around. Washington sat deep in meditation. Many in the room already had one hand on the bait that Henry had laid out for them.

Henry continued weaving his oral net. "The battle is not to the strong alone. It is to the vigilant, the active, the brave. It is too late to retire from the contest. There is no retreat but in submission and slavery. Our chains are forged. Their clanking may be heard on the plains of Boston!" Henry's entire body shook as he raised a fist upward. "The war is inevitable. And let it come. I repeat it, sir, let it come!"

Rumbles of "peace, peace" rose up around Pendleton, who nodded in agreement.

"Gentlemen may cry, 'peace, peace,' but there is no peace." Henry smirked. "The war is actually begun. The next gale that sweeps from the north will bring to our ears the clash of resounding arms! Our brethren are already in the field. Why stand we here idle?" Henry took two steps back and delivered an impressive pause.

"Is life so dear, or peace so sweet, as to be purchased at the price of chains and slavery?" Henry bowed his head and crossed his wrists as if a condemned slave. Then, with wrists still crossed, he raised head and hands toward heaven with a mighty shout. "Forbid it, Almighty God!" He bent slowly toward the earth as if under the weight of additional chains. "I know not what course others may take." He raised his form upward, his voice echoing as his arms spread wide and he loosed the imaginary chains. "But as for me, give me liberty"—he plucked his paper cutter from his pocket and, as if a dagger, held it out before his chest and plunged it toward his heart—"or give me death!"

Silence.

Pendleton's breathing grew shallow.

Minutes passed.

Then a rustling came from outside one of the open windows. Pendleton turned toward the sound. A young man who had been listening to the speech stuck his head through the opening and cried, "Let me be buried at this spot!"

Lee found his feet. "I will but remind those who have cautioned us against moving forward that the race is not to the swift, nor the battle to the strong or even to the wise, but to those whose cause is just."

"I concur with Mr. Henry and Mr. Lee."

Pendleton stirred at the sound of Jefferson's voice.

"And I believe," Jefferson said, "it is time to move forward with what has been proposed."

If Henry's words could cause Jefferson to speak publicly, not once, but twice in the same meeting, who knew how far his gift of persuasion had reached?

Pendleton rose to his feet. "Gentlemen, Mr. Henry has given a heartfelt speech that will resonate with many. Yet if ever there was a time that we should let our heads, rather than our hearts, guide us, 'tis now. It is the only way to victory."

Thomas Nelson Jr. stood.

Tension flowed out of Pendleton, and a corner of his mouth lifted. At last, a friend.

"Mr. President," Nelson said. "As this body is aware, I have been slow to consider war as a viable option. However, I am now ready to let my trade perish, and although the militia has already been preparing, I believe it is time to declare our plans publicly rather than hide them under a bushel." Nelson turned to Pendleton. "Gentlemen, with God as my witness, if any British troops should be landed in my county, I and those over whom I have command will do our utmost to repel them at the water's edge, regardless of whether I have received orders to do so."

What? Even Nelson was ready to switch sides?

If this ship could not be turned around, the words of Henry's resolutions must at least be softened. Pendleton addressed the delegates. "May I propose, Mr. President, that the resolutions be amended, ever so slightly, to read 'Resolved, therefore, *as the opinion of this convention*, that this colony *ought to be* put in a posture of defense.'" Would they push back against wording that might prevent the formation of a committee and, in practice, prevent the resolutions from having their intended outcome?

President Randolph cleared his throat and gazed over Pendleton's head to the others. "Gentlemen, the time has come to take a vote on Mr. Henry's resolutions. As they were originally presented."

Pendleton braced himself. Maybe, just maybe, enough conservatives would stand firm.

The vote came to the floor, and Henry's resolutions passed by a mere five votes. He was named chairman of the committee, with Lee as his second. Others would round out the majority while Pendleton and his followers would represent the minority.

The winds had shifted once again. Henry and his allies had won the day. Pendleton sunk back against the pew and stared into the mass of humanity mingling about him.

His country must be brought back from the brink of war. Liberty *could* be preserved without requiring the colonists to pay the ultimate price. He would protect those he represented. In time, the fervor stirred by Henry's oration would fade, then he would lead his fellow delegates back to reason. He clutched the railing in front of him. A few days at his in-laws' place in Goochland would allow time for reflection before heading back to the busyness of his plantation and expected return to Philadelphia.

Henry's reckless ways must be stopped.

CHAPTER 9

Gunpowder

May 2, 1775

The urgent message had reversed the course of Henry and his two traveling companions as they traveled northward toward Philadelphia. Now retracing the few miles back home to Hanover County, Virginia, the three men had found their stride amid the clippety-clop of their horses' hooves beneath them. Rays from the early May sun warmed Henry's face, and his spirit danced with joy at the news. "It is a most fortunate circumstance, wouldn't you say?"

Henry's cousin, a member of the Hanover County committee, crinkled his nose. "You would call the governor removing the arms and ammunition from their storage in Williamsburg fortunate?"

Henry nodded as he ran his fingers through his horse's mane. "Who could expect the people to concern themselves over the tax on tea? They do not understand how it will affect them. But tell them of the robbery of the magazine and that the next step will be to remove their weapons, and they will be ready to fly to arms to defend their independence."

The colonel, four years Henry's senior and also a member of Hanover's committee, nodded. "The response of those who have heard Lord Dunmore's words indicate they do not accept the justification he has given."

An involuntary grunt escaped from Henry's mouth. "Removing the very things that are meant to protect us, then claiming the action was for our own good. Why would anyone believe that?"

Silence settled upon the three men. As Newcastle's river-port-town approached, neighbor to Henry's boyhood home, the familiar scent of peonies tingled Henry's senses. The winding Pamunkey River floating by brought back memories of him and his cousin canoeing down one of its tributaries during their carefree days of childhood. How times had changed.

The colonel nodded at the slaves tilling the soil of nearby fields in preparation for planting tobacco. "Lord Dunmore claims rumors of an insurrection by the slaves in a neighboring county drove him to do it, and that providing powder for armed citizens would merely make the situation worse."

Henry tightened the grip on his horse's reins. "While at the same time claiming he will provide the arms and ammunition within a half hour of our demanding them. None of it makes sense."

His cousin laughed. "Lord Dunmore spewed excuses in an apparent attempt to convince the people that something other than fear for himself and his family was the reason. Your declaration of liberty or death a few weeks ago, not to mention the raising of a militia, has turned more than a few heads." A sheepish grin spread across his cousin's face. "Some say it was your words that prompted the governor's actions and subsequent threats."

The muscles in Henry's neck tightened. "Lord Dunmore's tactic of fighting fear with fear, by claiming he'll arm the slaves and reduce Williamsburg to ashes, shall not deter us."

"And don't forget the warning by the captain of the ship where the munitions are stored," the colonel said. "The people of Yorktown are on edge at the thought of being fired upon."

The camp of young men who had gathered at Newcastle came into view. "Whoa." Henry pulled on his horse's reins. His chest swelled with pride at the sight of the town his surveyor father had laid out around the time of Patrick's birth.

The three men pulled their horses to a stop. Nearly two hundred of Hanover's volunteers stretched out before them, awaiting their marching orders.

Henry nodded to his riding companions. "Thank you, gentlemen, for allowing me to share my thoughts. It seems that Providence retrieved me from my journey. I am obviously needed here more than in Philadelphia. We will hold our governor accountable, and his actions will serve us well toward our ultimate separation from the grip of the Motherland. After I speak with the committee, and upon their swift approval, we will be ready to advance."

More than six hundred militiamen gathered at Fredericksburg, Virginia, sat poised to march on Williamsburg, recover the gunpowder, and secure the magazine. For Pendleton and his traveling companions, the journey north would have to wait. Armed with rifles and tomahawks and clad in "Liberty or Death" uniforms, it seemed every man in the county, whether rich or poor, had turned out. Guiding their mounts toward the marquee tent, Pendleton, Randolph, and Harrison wove in and out of men whose snippets of conversations floated by.

"My spring crops aren't gonna plant themselves," one man grumbled.

"Where's your sense of adventure?" another asked.

A third man stretched full length, rested his chin on his knuckles, and spoke up. "You ain't got a pregnant wife back home or you wouldn't ask."

At the tent, the men dismounted, turned their horses over to others for safe keeping, and walked through the open flap. An aide-de-camp rose to welcome them.

"Major Hugh Mercer will be with you shortly," the aide said. "As a member of Fredericksburg's Committee of Safety and member of the town's Independent Company of volunteers, he will be able to provide you with updates." The aide disappeared through the tent's opening, leaving the three delegates alone once again.

Pendleton reached out to Randolph, who had arrived at Edmundsbury ill. "How are you feeling?"

Randolph shrugged. "Not well, but better."

Pendleton squeezed Randolph's forearm. "You let us know if there is anything you need. Anything."

Noise from the tent's entrance drew the men's attention, and the major entered. Limiting introductions, the delegates quickly moved to reviewing all that had transpired in the town during the days before their arrival.

"I must tell you," Major Mercer said, "when your letters urging the men to return home reached our camp, there was quite the uprising. A month's worth of drills had readied the men for action. But while all are hearty souls and ready to fight, some dread the horrors of a civil war and desperately wish to heal our mutual wounds with England through peaceable measures. At least as long as any hope of reconciliation remains."

The tension eased in Pendleton's shoulders. "Very wise. Of course, with the rumors coming out of Boston—"

"Until those rumors are confirmed," Randolph said, "we will make our decisions based on the assurance I received from Lord Dunmore before I left Williamsburg. He plans to return the gunpowder, which should restore tranquility."

"Colonel Washington also advised us against marching to the capital," Major Mercer said.

"Violence," Pendleton said, "could lead to serious consequences. Until further notice, we will continue to offer a soft answer in hopes it will turn away wrath."

Randolph nodded. "The governor considers his honor at stake. If left to himself, I believe he will cheerfully do as he should and return the powder. He assured me of this privately. If he feels forced, however, he may push back in ways none of us desire."

"Nonetheless," Pendleton said, "the militia should be kept ready until we learn more about the rumors from Boston."

The major shuffled a few papers on his makeshift desk, handing one over for the men to read. "Here is what my men agreed to. Starting there." He pointed as Randolph accepted the paper.

Randolph's eyes narrowed as he studied the paper, then he read aloud. "'But considering the just rights of and liberty of America to be greatly endangered and being firmly resolved to resist such attempts at the utmost hazard of our lives and fortunes, we do now pledge ourselves to each other to be in readiness at a moment's warning, to reassemble, and by force of arms to defend the laws, the liberty, and rights of this or any sister colony, from unjust and wicked invasion.'"

"I like 'readiness at a moment's warning,'" Pendleton said. "At this stage, preparedness with restraint is best. We should send dispatches to other counties where militia have gathered, telling them of your decision. Please include Caroline County. Even though Mr. Randolph and I asked them to remain calm and return home, they need to be reassured that others are doing the same. My committee has secured gunpowder for them in recent days, so they are ready. Mr. Randolph has already written to those gathered in Hanover County, encouraging them to return home."

Randolph stood and placed the piece of paper on the desk, then turned to Major Mercer. "Shall we inform the men of your gracious offer?"

While the others moved to the exit of the marquee, Pendleton's eyes followed the paper to the desk. Then he saw it. At the bottom of the page. Rather than "God save the King," it read "God Save the Liberties of America." He tucked the words away in his mind for further study while the men exited the tent to join the hundreds who awaited their words of instruction.

The militiamen stirred as their leader came into view.

Major Mercer mounted a horse to get everyone's attention. "Men," the major shouted. "We will march after all!"

A mix of cheers and groans went up from the throng of men.

"But it will not be to Williamsburg."

Looks of confusion met the announcement.

"Instead," Major Mercer said, "we will provide a military escort for our fine delegates as they journey to the Grand Congress in Philadelphia. We will protect them since our very own Lord Dunmore has ordered county magistrates to prevent what he calls an unjustifiable proceeding. Men, prepare to travel to the Potomac where we will bid the delegates adieu. We depart at daybreak."

"Hip, hip!" someone cried.

"Huzzah!" the response came.

The camp shifted into action as assistants led Pendleton, Randolph, and Harrison to their overnight quarters.

The matter had been settled. Williamsburg would remain calm while they journeyed to meet up with Colonel Washington and other delegates. Henry would catch up to them after receiving Randolph's plea for calm and restraint.

The late afternoon sun greeted Henry as he thrust open and marched out the door. He paced the short distance, across the earth's dusty soil, to provide the troops with an answer. Waiting had never been Henry's strong suit, but the Hanover committee refused to be rushed in responding to his proposal to march the men sixty miles to Williamsburg to either collect the stolen goods or obtain restitution for them. The volunteers, with "Liberty or Death" stitched boldly upon their shirts, mingled in the street. Tomahawks hung by their side.

A bronze sun brushed the horizon as Henry scanned the area for a platform. The bench would do. He leapt upon it. "Gather round, and I will prepare you for what lies ahead."

The buzz of excitement turned to a sense of anticipation. All eyes turned to Henry.

"Men," he began, "for years, the British Ministry has sought to reduce the colonies to subjection by robbing them of all means of defending their rights."

"Hear, hear!" someone shouted.

Henry squinted against the encroaching darkness to see the many faces that surrounded him. "Even now, we hear of blood flowing in the streets of Lexington and Concord—blood shed for our cause. Was not the recent plunder of the magazine in our capital an attempt at subjugation? The time has come for us to choose whether we will live free and hand down the noble inheritance to our children or to become servants of a tyrannical ministry."

"We won't have it!" a man from the crowd shouted.

"Not here!" another one cried.

Passionate faces glowed as flames from torches began to dot the landscape. Men who had spent the day with a pitchfork, plow, or hoe now raised their guns heavenward in an act of defiance.

A smile spread across Henry's face. "The promised land of liberty can be won by your valor under the support and guidance of heaven."

He gazed intently into the crowd before him. "Though this might lead us through a sea of blood, we must remember the same God whose power parted the Red Sea is still the enemy of the oppressor and the friend of the oppressed."

Shouts of agreement went up from the small army, one voice rising above the rest. "Let the one who speaks be our Moses and lead us to the promised land!"

Henry raised one hand, his voice reaching a crescendo. "No time should be lost. If we act by a rapid and vigorous movement, we can restore the powder that has been carried off. Or else obtain payment from the king's coffers to balance the account of goods taken. Either provides the Hanover Volunteers with the opportunity to strike the first blow in this colony in the great cause of American liberty and receive never-fading laurels."

"Hurrah!" the men cheered.

Delight swelled up within Henry before he noticed the captain of Hanover County's Independent Company. He, the fierce Indian fighter, was the rightful leader of Hanover militia. If Henry accepted the role of Moses, would the crowd view it as an act of mutiny? His mind raced. Had he let the moment carry him along without giving it enough thought?

The captain made his way to the front and stood beside the bench. "Gentlemen, I gladly submit my resignation to make room for Moses —Mr. Patrick Henry. Dare I say Captain Henry?"

The men cheered, slapping each other on the back.

Henry mouthed a heartfelt thank-you.

Another man stepped forward waving the modified hunting shirt, turned popular Virginia uniform, above his head. Fringe dangled from its waist. The man grabbed the shoulders of the canvas shirt and held up its inscription for all to see. "Let the one who uttered these words, 'Liberty or Death,' lead us to victory." The man flashed a broad smile at Henry, then presented him with the uniform. "We await your orders, Captain." His fist shot into the air. "Huzzah!"

Henry had captured their imagination.

Smoke from the campfire drifted toward the star-filled sky. Henry's men encamped several paces away, a few still milling about as if in anticipation of what lie ahead. The harmonious singing of crickets and frogs seemed in sharp contrast to the military drills of earlier in the day. The new commander pushed one boot against the ground, causing the log beneath him to wobble. He paused, casting a blank stare into the flames. Sarah had loved nights like this. At least she could no longer fret over his ventures—

"You sent for me?" Parke Goodall's voice echoed into the night air.

"Yes." Henry scrambled to his feet. "Thank you for standing with me in this."

"Of course," Goodall said.

Henry gripped Goodall's shoulder with one hand as he retrieved the paper from his coat pocket with the other. "You must leave tonight. I have sixteen men ready to accompany you." He held out the sealed document. "Here are your orders, only to be opened enroute to Laneville."

Henry nodded south. "Godspeed to you, my friend. I will see you soon."

Goodall turned to go, but Henry grabbed his arm. "When you complete your mission, you can find me and the volunteers on the road to the capital."

CHAPTER 10

Satisfaction

May 3 - 11, 1775

Henry smiled, and the horse beneath him snorted. Behind them, songs of liberty blasted forth from the fife and drums, followed by more than a hundred men. The trip to Williamsburg had become more of a parade than battle march. Townsfolk lined the route, cheering at the Hanover Volunteers' cries of patriotism.

Dust stirred as a horse-mounted aide reached Henry's side. "I beg your pardon, sir, but another messenger has arrived from the governor."

A young man, mounted upon a horse, paused behind the aide.

Henry swallowed the frustration that threatened to escape his lips. "Do you bring the same message as those who have come before?"

"If they conveyed Lord Dunmore's desire that you turn back from your advance toward the capital, then yes, sir, I do."

Henry motioned with his head to one of the nearby soldiers. "Please take this messenger to join the others."

"But," the courier objected, "the governor will expect me to return with a report."

"And why would I want to provide Lord Dunmore with any more intelligence than necessary, through you or any of the others he has sent?" Henry flicked his fingers toward the men. "Take him away."

The messenger held up a hand. "You should also know that the governor has armed his slaves and threats to destroy the capital, if you continue your march there."

"I understand." Henry nodded toward the rear, and the messenger galloped away with his escort, leaving Henry to collect his thoughts. His company of men, now joined by militia from other counties, had more than doubled since their dawn departure. They cheered at the news that the village of New Kent Courthouse had voted to prepare their arms for a possible emergency. Yet the lack of word from Goodall overshadowed all else. Hours crawled by with no word. Had his mission been a success or a failure?

In late afternoon, Doncastle's Ordinary finally came into view. The tavern and its surrounds would provide for their needs. Henry swung his horse around and held up a hand, ordering the march to halt. "Men, this is where we'll set up camp until we receive additional news."

Segments of the militiamen began preparing for the evening, while others soaked in the stillness after a day's ride.

Henry dismounted, handing over the reins to an orderly. His muscles rejoiced at the opportunity to stretch a bit. As the commissary saw to it that the men received the necessary refreshment, Henry sent word to the company in Yorktown. The men there needed to prevent reinforcements from making their way from the Royal Navy warship *Fowley* to Williamsburg and also prevent the governor from taking refuge aboard the Man of War sitting in the James River.

Task complete, Henry kicked at the dirt. Long shadows of evening had fallen across the encampment, and still no word.

"Look, Captain Henry." One of his men pointed over Henry's shoulder.

Henry turned, this time northward, to see yet another messenger arriving. Surely this latest arrival would provide him with the long-awaited news. But did the horseman's blond hair mean . . . ?

Yes, indeed, 'twas Carter Braxton, son-in-law of Richard Corbin, the king's receiver general to whom Henry had sent Goodall the night before. The latest messenger came to a standstill beside Henry. Braxton's refined manners did little to ease past tensions between them, as a fellow burgess or otherwise. Henry raised an eyebrow.

The young man stared down at Henry. "I know of your plans and desire to give you additional intelligence which may deter you and your men from your march."

Henry gave Braxton a narrow-eyed look. "Oh?"

"I was in Caroline County yesterday where I observed three of your colleagues convince the militia there to refrain from marching on Williamsburg. They were going to stop by Fredericksburg to do the same." Braxton pulled on the reins of his snorting horse. "On the strength of that precedent, I would encourage you to do the same."

"Am I to assume Colonel Pendleton was among this group?" Henry's voice emerged gruff and low.

Braxton nodded. "Along with the Speaker and Mr. Harrison. They are journeying to Philadelphia together."

"I am sure you are aware I do not always see things the same way they do."

"Your zeal is commendable," Braxton said. "However, the mobbish manner in which you tend to carry out your desires needs to be tamed. Word from Lexington and Concord indicates the people there were in a state of *defense*. You appear ready to *attack*."

Henry smirked. "Thank you, but I will be the judge of my own actions." Movement in the distance caught Henry's eye, then he motioned to the orderly who had appeared at Braxton's arrival. "Please tend to Colonel Braxton's mount." Henry took several steps toward the new arrival, before turning back to Braxton. "Please wait inside the tavern until I am ready to continue our conversation."

Braxton headed to the tavern while Henry remained outside. With footsteps fading behind him, his heartbeat quickened at the sight of Goodall. Henry's mind raced in anticipation of what news his friend might carry with him. No prisoner seemed to be among them. Perhaps the men had indeed obtained compensation from the receiver general for the stolen goods.

As soon as Goodall's horse came to a stop, he launched in, taking no time for niceties. "We found out at dawn that Colonel Corbin was not at home. His wife says he is in the capital."

Twenty-four hours of waiting, only to receive no answer. Henry motioned to the building.

"Carter Braxton is inside."

Goodall's eyes shot open.

A cloud of dust and the arrival of yet another messenger drew Henry's attention. A few minutes of exchange, then Henry and Goodall entered the tavern. On the other side of the room, Braxton heaved himself up from the chair. Henry and Goodall weaved in and out of the few patrons lingering over bowls of soup and bread. Slurping and muffled conversations behind them, Henry remained standing to encourage a brief exchange.

"Mr. Braxton." Henry held up the piece of paper he had just received. "It seems your father-in-law received word of my request and has provided £330 in bills of exchange as restitution."

"I believed he would do you right," Braxton said.

"But I have refused to accept them."

Braxton shot Henry a questioning look.

"With the uncertain times, particularly with a warship sitting off the coast which could sweep away our beloved governor and all officials of the Crown who are still loyal to him, the paper could quickly become worthless. Unless, that is, someone more sympathetic to our cause would be willing to endorse it."

Braxton shifted his weight and looked away. "Perhaps I could obtain such a person for you in Williamsburg."

"Then Godspeed to you, Mr. Braxton. We will remain here until you have brought us word of the outcome of your mission. With the lateness of the hour, we will not expect you until morning." Henry glanced at Goodall, then back at Braxton. "Good day, gentlemen."

Henry's men had just begun to stir amid the morning light when he added his bold signature to the paper. Then he led Braxton back to the open tavern door. "Thank you, Mr. Braxton, for your part in this."

Braxton provided a curt nod and accepted the receipt as the two men exited the building. An orderly handed Braxton the reins to his horse.

"Deliver this letter to Mr. Nicholas," Henry said. "As Virginia's treasurer, I am certain he will want to know of my satisfaction with the settlement." He reached under his hunting shirt to the waistcoat pocket and pulled out a second document. "I am also offering our services to protect the public treasury, if he considers its current location to be one of danger."

Braxton accepted the document and mounted his horse.

"Have him send a messenger posthaste," Henry said, "so my men and I will know if we are needed further."

The weeklong journey to Philadelphia had resumed once again, and Henry's horse found its stride amid the large number of volunteers escorting him to the Potomac River. A hush settled over the small band, including Goodall, which led the way northward. Jubilant music from fifes and drums behind them faded while echoes of dissidence from the past week reverberated inside Henry's head.

No joy had been lost at the rejection of Henry's offer to protect the treasury. His men had returned home in triumph. Surely his colleagues in Congress would agree that justice had been done and restitutions made to the country for the insult it had received with the taking of the powder.

Yet Lord Dunmore's words haunted Henry. He shook his head. The march to Williamsburg had *not* been in defiance of the law, but if the governor wanted to look upon it as a posture of war, then so be it. The coward had waited until the threat to Virginia's capital had faded before spewing out his venomous words. No doubt, the people of his colony would not heed Lord Dunmore's charge to refuse aid to Henry but, instead, would oppose their governor by every means possible.

"Captain Henry," one of his escorts said, extending his hand toward a horseman who had just arrived. "May I present express rider James Madison, who has a message from his county."

"James Madison? Shall I assume the man I know by that name is your father?" Henry said, as the men continued to ride.

Madison nodded. "My father is the head of Orange County's Committee of Safety. I am his namesake."

"Ah, I, too, am a junior, though by my uncle." Although tempted, Henry suppressed the urge to judge Pendleton's Madison kinfolk without a fair trial. "How are things in Orange County? I trust you will relay my gratitude to those who took up arms in the recent cause."

"I will." Madison delivered a timid smile.

"How old are you, lad?"

"Twenty-four."

"And you bring a message for me?" Henry asked.

Madison fumbled in his pocket.

Henry tugged at the reins of his mount. "Mr. Madison, shall we give our horses a reprieve?"

The two men fell out of line with the others, then dismounted. Goodall took their reins, then motioned for the troops following them to come to a halt.

"Isn't this better?" Henry motioned to Madison's pocket. "Now, let's hear what your county has to say."

Madison retrieved the paper, then began to read aloud. Henry beamed. The flow of appreciation from multiple counties throughout the day may have slowed his progress northward, yet it warmed his soul.

"'We take this occasion,'" Madison continued, "'also to give it as our opinion that the blow struck in the Massachusetts Bay government is a hostile attack on this and every other colony, and a sufficient warrant to use violence and reprisal, in all cases where it may be expedient for our security and welfare.'" The young man raised his head.

"Bravo," Henry said, "and many thanks for your part in getting this message to me. If you can spare the time, I will provide a handwritten reply."

The corners of Madison's mouth turned up. "We would be much obliged. There is nothing more powerful than a blank piece of paper, wouldn't you say?"

Henry tilted his head to Madison and extended his hand to an orderly. "Please, enjoy a few moments of refreshment while I prepare the my reply."

Having written so many responses along the journey, the minutes passed quickly before Henry handed the letter to Madison.

The youth shuffled his feet and drew a piece of paper from his saddlebag. "If you would be so kind, I have written a brief note for you to carry to a college friend of mine in Philadelphia. I know some there may not understand your actions. Perhaps my words, small as they may be, would assure your colleagues that those back home commend you for what you have done."

"It will be no problem at all," Henry said.

With notes exchanged, Henry returned to his saddle where his doubts surfaced once again. He squeezed his writing hand. Had the letter written to Richard Henry Lee's brother Frank a few days before been necessary? Had it gone too far in defending his positions? No, he was right to counter arguments sure to surface at Virginia's next convention. While Henry was in Philadelphia, Frank would defend his cause at home. The gunpowder did *not* belong to the king, and the letter had laid out his case.

Henry cast a parting glimpse over his shoulder at Madison riding off in the distance. At least a dozen counties, even Caroline, had sent words of encouragement throughout the day, providing thanks to Henry for his conduct during the recent gunpowder affair. Had the tide finally turned in his favor?

The band of men regained its momentum as music rose up before him, then a ferry came into view.

Henry chuckled. "Well, gentlemen, it appears news of my arrival has proceeded me." He pulled back on the reins and motioned for Goodall to come aside to receive some parting words. "I cannot thank you enough for the protection you and the others have provided."

Goodall nodded. "Lord Dunmore's threat to arrest you should not extend to the other side of the river. You will be safe there."

"Thank you, too," Henry said, "for your listening ear."

"It has been a pleasure."

The two horsemen rejoined the others who escorted them to the river. Henry boarded the ferry amid repeated huzzahs from two platoons. Maryland uniformed volunteers waited on the opposite shore to provide assistance on the next leg of his journey to Philadelphia.

What kind of reception would greet him there?

CHAPTER 11

𝕿𝖍𝖊 𝕾𝖜𝖔𝖗𝖉 𝖆𝖓𝖉 𝖙𝖍𝖊 𝕺𝖑𝖎𝖛𝖊 𝕭𝖗𝖆𝖓𝖈𝖍

MAY 9 - 26, 1775

Pendleton pulled back on his horse's reins at the messenger's words, the weariness of the journey forgotten. "Mr. Henry did *what*?"

The express rider nodded to Pendleton, then glanced at the half dozen delegates atop their horses. "He decided to march on Williamsburg. I left before the matter was settled, so I do not know the outcome."

The muscles in Pendleton's jaw tightened. "Mr. Randolph made it clear before we left Virginia that such measures could produce undesired consequences."

Randolph turned his horse to face the men. "Only God knows where Mr. Henry's actions could lead."

Pendleton surveyed the faces of his four fellow delegates from Virginia who had met up with the duo from North Carolina in Baltimore four days prior. None seemed too pleased with the message that had been delivered.

Washington was most difficult to read. "Had news of Lexington and Concord reached Mr. Henry?"

"I believe it had, sir."

Pendleton shook his head and caught Washington's eye. The two men understood New England's resistance, if not agitated, should open the door for conciliation. But Henry's latest faux pas simply magnified his lack of military experience and could jeopardize the chance for peace.

One of the North Carolina delegates spoke up. "Some of us are not yet ready to accept war and death as the only answer. I fear many, such as Mr. Henry, feel a patriotic glow which leaves them without the ability to reason with those of differing opinions."

Pendleton ducked his chin in agreement.

Washington turned to the express rider. "How many accompanied Mr. Henry?"

"It's hard to say." The messenger shrugged. "Maybe a few hundred."

The other North Carolina delegate spoke up. "When we passed through your colony and lodged at the tavern in Hanover, we heard talk that fifteen hundred men were under arms and ready to proceed to the capital."

At the mention of Henry's domain, Pendleton cringed. "We had hoped Mr. Henry's foolery would not impact reality."

Washington turned his horse back toward Philadelphia. "Perhaps we will learn more once we arrive. We should be there in time for dinner at City Tavern." He kicked his horse into a trot.

Pendleton gritted his teeth. "Don't worry," he said, patting his horse's neck, "I won't take it out on you." He took a deep breath before joining the colonel on the final leg of their journey to the City of Brotherly Love.

Pendleton stood on the edge of a street on Philadelphia's outskirts, surrounded by men of every occupation and station of life. Children scurried about, mothers straining their necks above the crowd to keep little ones within view. Tolling bells and distant thunder echoed the change in atmosphere.

Less than twenty-four hours in Philadelphia had left no doubt. The spirit and minds of the people had shifted.

Drums and fifes sounded every hour, and talk of war found its way onto the lips of those around him much more readily than it had six months before. He rolled his fingers into a ball as muscles throughout his body stiffened. *What of reconciliation?* Conversation at supper with Washington and others the previous evening had centered around how they might stop up the Delaware channel to prevent the king's ships from making their way to the city.

Military leaders, swords drawn, led the procession marching on the road before Pendleton and the other spectators. The two or three hundred men on horseback who followed made a statement: If more blood is to be shed, we are ready.

But are we? Foreign allies, additional arms, and other equipment must be secured before we engage in military conflict, which no one should be ready to accept as inevitable.

The New England delegation came into view as the procession continued to roll along. The Adams cousins along with two others, same as before. Pendleton squinted at the unfamiliar one. John Hancock? Frail yet stately. Rumors indicated Hancock had not always been onboard with the radicals, yet recent events in his own colony—including his need to flee from possible capture—would likely have modified his position. How would his presence, coupled with Benjamin Franklin's arrival from London, sway the other delegates?

A bead of sweat trickled down Pendleton's back. It promised to be a long, hot summer.

"Colonel Pendleton?"

Pendleton turned to see a lad smiling, yet pleading with his eyes. "Yes, I am he. May I help you?"

The lad's face relaxed. "I am happy to have found you. I work for a local gentleman who is in need of your legal advice."

"I see." Pendleton glanced back at the parade. With responsibilities and long hours of Congress sure to come, could he spare the time? Yes, his life was one of service. Time well spent. Sleep and other pleasures would have to wait. He turned to the lad and extended his hand. "Shall we find a quiet place to talk?" The two men zigzagged their way out of the crowd and into the long, hot—and busy—summer.

The morning's cool breeze, a nice change from the day of the parade, accompanied Pendleton down the cobblestone streets to a new day of meetings. Two blocks west of Carpenters' Hall, the towering cupola atop Pennsylvania's State House had welcomed the delegates to their new meeting place. Pendleton suppressed a yawn. Despite a late night of providing legal services, a fresh energy lifted his spirit upon entering the large, two-story building. The center of Pennsylvania's government was the appropriate place for political debates. Surely the aura of the king's presence would temper any talks of rebellion against him.

Pendleton had found his spot and settled in. He rubbed his palms against the smooth arms of the Windsor chair. A table, inkwell, and quill, already in place, sat before him. A nice benefit to their new meeting space. Although shared with a couple of his fellow Virginia delegates, it would provide a spot for taking notes and more discretion when rubbing his weary limbs. Pendleton's eyelids drooped low. A couple days of military drills and warlike music by Philadelphia's companies at five o'clock in the morning were taking their toll. They, coupled with a few quick consultations before proceeding to the main assembly, did nothing to ward off the drowsiness brought on by endless hours of sitting.

Delegates mingled about the room, taking advantage of the morning's much needed break to interact with those who stood both for and against his own point of view. That would come soon enough for Pendleton. For now, he would continue to process the newness surrounding him. Chairs graced the additional two rows of tables spread in a slight arc from left to right across the room, windows at either end already draped shut for privacy. The president's chair faced the delegates on the other side of a table at the front of the room, flanked by a fireplace on each side.

With Randolph once again at the helm, Congress would be guided back to reason. And the decision to open this Congress with prayers provided additional hope.

Who would have thought instructions to the delegates from the Province of Massachusetts Bay by their own legislative body would provide some relief amid all the talk of war? The instructions counseled its representatives to "do what is needed to restore harmony between Great Britain and the colonies." Instructions to other colonies reflected similar sentiments. Yet a nagging truth undercut any encouragement they might otherwise provide, for they had been given prior to the news from Lexington and Concord.

Pendleton fixed his gaze on the clerk's workspace at the front of the room. The clerk's reading of other documents that morning threatened to brush away any promise of restoration with the Motherland. The letter provided by Benjamin Franklin, agent for the colonies to London, made it clear Britain had no plans to accept the colonists' petition. Not only had Parliament cast aside concerns of their local businessmen and rejected a motion to withdraw troops from Boston, they had ordered reinforcements to depart for America. Three regiments of foot, one of dragoons, seven hundred marines, two frigates, and six sloops of war. A knot formed in Pendleton's chest.

He double-tapped the table, stood, then paced off the short distance to the document-scattered lectern. Pendleton held out his hand to the clerk. "May I review the packet of materials presented this morning by Massachusetts Bay delegate John Hancock?"

With the packet in hand, Pendleton turned around and sauntered to a table pushed against the nearby wall. He set down the packet, then leaned over to examine its letter of introduction, which picked up where Franklin's letter left off:

A considerable reinforcement from Great Britain is daily expected in this colony, and we are now reduced to the sad alternative of defending ourselves by arms or submitting to be slaughtered.

We suggest that a powerful army be considered by this Congress as the only means left to stem the rapid progress of a tyrannical ministry. Without a force superior to our enemies, we must reasonably expect to become the victims of their relentless fury. With such a force, we may still have hopes of seeing an immediate end put to the inhuman ravages of mercenary troops in America and the wicked authors of our miseries brought to condign punishment by the just indignation of our brethren in Great Britain.

What followed—the threat to Massachusetts Bay's port towns by the potential approach of the so-called enemy by way of the sea— pushed Pendleton's mind to his own colony. Enemy or not, families were fleeing amid fear of the destruction warships could cause. If the conflict could draw Virginia in, she could be exposed to the same threat. Norfolk, while not on the scale of Boston with regards to size, provided Viginia with a portal to the other colonies and to the rest of the world. Already two royal ships sat in the James River, close enough to Virginia's port city to generate concern.

Massachusetts Bay ended the letter with a thinly-veiled plea for support, for the sake of the common cause.

"This session will come back to order." Randolph's voice reverberated behind Pendleton.

He pivoted to see the clerk coming to reclaim the packet, and everyone returned to their seats.

"The clerk," Randolph said, "will read the twenty depositions collected in the days following the atrocities at Lexington and Concord. These are eyewitness accounts and should provide additional details related to the time surrounding these events."

Over the years, many depositions had crossed Pendleton's desk, yet some required more mental and emotional preparation to read than others. He pressed his lips together, then rested each hand on a chair's arm. He gave a narrow-eyed look toward the front of the room. Ready.

The clerk began to read aloud. One after another carried the common theme: The king's troops outnumbered local militias and fired first, killing at least a half dozen and wounding many more. Each of the dead and wounded had a mother or other family who would feel the loss. For the rest of their lives.

"'Deposition Number Eighteen,'" the clerk read. "'Hannah Bradish testifies that about five o'clock on Wednesday afternoon, being in her bedchamber with her infant child, about eight-days-old, she was surprised by the firing of the king's troops on their return from Concord.'"

Pendleton froze. A young mother. With an eight-day-old infant. The words pierced a bruise in Pendleton's heart, a place he had protected for years.

The clerk continued. "'She soon found the house surrounded with the king's troops and, after they went off, observed at least seventy bullets were shot into the front part of the house. One passed through an easy chair she had gone from, and several personal items were missing, including a rich brocade gown, three caps, and one case of ivory knives.'"

Pendleton closed his eyes and thanked the Lord for sparing her and her family, and that the husband and father could hold them close even now. Grateful though he was for the wife and surrogate children now in his life, his heart would forever bear a scar from losing his first bride and their infant child. Death begat pain in those left behind. If he could prevent the former, then he could save untold numbers from experiencing the latter.

Glancing around, Pendleton assured himself that his visit to the past had gone undetected. Recomposed, he listened as the clerk read the closing letter from Massachusetts Bay, wrapping up their packet of materials.

"'These, brethren,'" the clerk read, "'are marks of a ministerial vengeance against this colony for refusing, with her sister colonies, a submission to slavery, but they have not yet detached us from our royal Sovereign. We profess to be his loyal and dutiful subjects. Nevertheless, to the persecution and tyranny of his cruel ministry, we will not tamely submit. Appealing to heaven for the justice of our cause, we determine to die or be free.'"

To die or be free. Similar words had touched Pendleton's ears a few weeks before. Words from Patrick Henry's own lips. Would the impending arrival of his fellow Virginian in Philadelphia add fuel to the Massachusetts Bay fire?

"Are you sure about this?" Pendleton asked his twenty-year-old nephew packing the portmanteau laid out on the cot. Aroma from the dark brown leather bag permeated the tent. "If it is the accommodations . . ."

Jack Taylor pulled his arms away from his task and motioned to the dwelling's vaulted roof. "The marquee is no problem. It is as fine as any brick house in Philadelphia. On this matter, our paths simply diverge." He slumped onto his cot and shrugged.

Pendleton rubbed his cot's blanket on which he sat, then looked to the floor, making note that one of the duckboards had already worked loose. "With all the losses I have experienced in my life, everything within me wants to protect you and others from possible harm. It's one of the reasons I am here now. So I must say, I know there are many who have contracted smallpox through natural means, but to have it injected into your body by choice . . ."

Jack stood and resumed packing. "The inoculation should only place me in quarantine a couple weeks or so, then I shall return ready to resume my lessons." Jack turned to Pendleton. "You didn't seem to have a problem with Mr. Henry getting inoculated."

"Mr. Henry is a different case," Pendleton chuckled. "His inability to participate in Congress has been a gift from above."

A grin spread across Jack's face. "I thought you said the rules of Congress would keep him confined."

"To some degree." Pendleton pushed himself from the cot and to his feet. "It was no accident that Congress reviewed our methods of procedure on Mr. Henry's first day back. He could still speak, just not control the debate."

"If whispers on the streets of Philadelphia can be believed, Mr. Henry's rashness has lost him the confidence and esteem of most sensible men."

"Jack," Pendleton said, "I must be clear. My differences with Mr. Henry are not personal. He is a fine man and full of zeal. But that zeal often rushes ahead before he has taken time to think through the consequences of his words."

"Many agree with you." Jack rolled the top of his bag closed, fastened down the straps, then sank back into his cot. "I will certainly give him your regards if I see him."

"You do that." Pendleton walked over to his makeshift desk and shuffled a few papers. He handed one of them to Jack. "You may gift him with this newspaper from me. He can read all about our victory at Fort Ticonderoga in New York. He arrived in Congress just in time to hear about it, but he has been known to brush aside important details."

Jack laid the newspaper on top of his bag. "How many cannon did the militia recover?"

"Two hundred cannon and a significant amount of gunpowder—items the British had seized in Boston." Looking down on the young man, whom he had raised as his own, brought back a flood of memories. Where had the time gone? "You are a good student, Jack. It has been a joy to have you along on this trip."

Jack patted the newspaper. "Wasn't this the edition that contained reports from Mr. Henry's march to Williamsburg?"

"Yes, it is. Fortunately, other things have Congress' attention right now. As for Virginia, Mr. Randolph will act wisely at the upcoming convention with regards to Mr. Henry's behavior in handling the issue with the gunpowder the governor seized. I recommended that the convention not censure him."

"I thought Mr. Randolph was presiding over Congress, here in Philadelphia."

"He was until he announced his intention to return to Virginia to oversee its convention. Yesterday, Congress elected John Hancock of Massachusetts Bay to take Mr. Randolph's place while he is away. Sorry, but with the long days and short nights, I have not had the opportunity to tell you."

Jack wrapped his fingers around the bag's handle and slid to the edge of the cot. "Do you think you will be pleased with Mr. Hancock?"

"We are at a critical crossroads." Pendleton took a step back, making room for Jack.

Jack hoisted himself to his feet, bag in tow. "You are afraid your resolves won't pass, aren't you?"

Pendleton nodded and escorted Jack to the exit. "The debate has been intense, and Congress will eventually need to come down on one side or the other. I fear a decision might come before reason has had a chance to take hold of some of the more radical factions, including Mr. Henry."

The debate inside the Pennsylvania State House mirrored the rising temperatures outside. Pendleton fingered the papers on the table in front of him which contained his proposed resolves. Throughout the day, delegates had debated varying perspectives as to what Congress' next step should be.

Richard Henry Lee now held the floor. "Raising an army," he boldly proclaimed, "is our only way forward. We must prepare for war."

"Before we can even entertain the question of raising an army," a delegate from South Carolina said, "shouldn't we first determine if independence is what we aim for?"

John Adams jumped out of his seat. "Must I remind this body that during the meetings of the first Congress last year we settled that argument? We agreed that the English constitution already provides for the colonies' independence from Parliament."

John Dickinson of Pennsylvania rose. Pendleton cast him an encouraging glance. Several years before, Pendleton had read Dickinson's *Letters from a Farmer* articles with great interest. Now, the two men fought side by side in the battle for moderation.

"While I agreed with Lee's proposal to *prepare* for war," Dickinson said, "I believe other options must be considered before rushing into it. Without reiterating every point I laid out to this body three days ago, I will remind you of the options I believe we have. One, we send our American agents back to London to negotiate a settlement, perhaps even offering to pay for the tea that was destroyed in Boston's harbor. Two of my options include preparing for war, one would include a simultaneous petition to the king."

"But the king ignored our previous petition," someone said. "Why would we expect him to respond any differently to a subsequent one?"

Pendleton leaned forward in his chair. *Patience. Time. Restraint.*

"As for preparing for war while sending another petition," John Adams chimed in, "I do not believe it is possible to hold the sword in one hand and the olive branch in the other."

Pendleton stood. "Gentlemen, so many good thoughts have been presented by the fine representatives we have among us." He turned to catch the eye of each one present, providing a nod to Lee. "It is both prudent and wise for us, as members of this present Congress, to support each other in defense of American liberty while, at the same time, seeking reconciliation with our Mother Country. Both can, and must, be done.

"Yet we must keep firmly in mind," he continued, "that the present unhappy dispute between the British Ministry, Parliament, and America is not an inclination on our part for independence."

Pendleton scanned the closing remarks of his resolves in front of him before looking back to his colleagues. "To this desirable end—that the troops may be withdrawn from us and the several acts of Parliament repealed—we will do away with all associations and other things disgusting to our brethren in Britain." Pendleton paused as months of wrestling unfolded before him. "But if there is no choice left us but absolute submission to the mandates of a British Ministry or resistance, we are determined to embrace the latter. And we will pursue it to the last period of our breath, appealing to heaven for the justice and rectitude of our intentions. And trusting in the Almighty for our protection and defense." Pendleton returned to his chair and committed the results to the Sovereign Lord.

After more debate, the final resolutions were read, and Pendleton soaked in the key points. The battles at Lexington and Concord had placed them in a dangerous and critical situation. The resolutions pleaded for a restoration of harmony between the Mother Country and the colonies. And they agreed to petition the king to negotiate regarding the unhappy disputes that had come between him and the colonies.

Although Pendleton's head accepted the most glaring of the resolutions—a vow to put all of the colonies in a state of defense—his heart continued to resist where such a public commitment might lead. Would this resolution prove too difficult to implement, or would Congress find a way to make it happen? Pendleton braced himself for the coming days, knowing the answer was sure to come.

A State of Defense

June 1775

$\mathfrak{P}$endleton scanned the courtyard as he made his way to the Pennsylvania State House. His many years as a burgess had fine-tuned his ability to recognize secret negotiations when he saw them. John and Samuel Adams's conversation seemed particularly intense under June's morning sun. The duo's ability to sway the body of delegates had been impressive, but would it be enough to overcome today's deliberations?

Now, with the opening prayer and other ceremonies behind them and the previous day's vote to raise six companies of expert riflemen, Pendleton held little doubt for what the debate would center around. A glimpse back at Washington's spot near the door confirmed what everyone in Congress had come to expect: his full blue and buff military attire, a relic from his days of fighting against the French and Indians. Today, Pendleton and the others were prepared for the battle of the minds.

A scraping coming from a sliding chair at the Massachusetts Bay table drew the attention of the delegates. As John Adams rose, he thanked President Hancock for giving him the opportunity to speak. Adams's cousin shifted in his seat.

"Gentlemen," John Adams began, "as most of you are willing to admit, Britain has placed these colonies in a dangerous state of affairs. The people are anxious, and I get regular reports that it will be impossible to keep together those who seek to defend us. That is, unless Congress offers its assistance."

Adams pivoted to face the southern delegation. "Our delaying the inevitable would furnish Britain with a great advantage. My colony has experienced it firsthand. We can wait no longer. The time has come for more serious preparations. And so, I motion that Congress adopt the army that is currently based in Cambridge and appoint a general."

Without movement, Pendleton caught a glimpse of Hancock from the corner of his eye. A smile tugged at the corners of the president's lips. Had the Adamses decided to nominate one of their own? Pendleton's intuition said no. But then why Hancock's apparent glee?

Adams turned toward the front of the room. "I have no hesitation to declare that I have but one gentleman in mind for that important command. And it is a gentleman from Virginia."

Hancock's countenance fell.

"He is among us," Adams said, "and very well known."

A shuffle came from the back of the room. Pendleton turned to see Washington leaving the meeting. The pace of Pendleton's heartbeat quickened.

The Massachusetts Bay delegate continued. "This gentleman is skilled and experienced as an officer. His independent fortune, great talents, and excellent universal character would command praise of all Americans and unite the colonies better than any other person in this union."

Samuel Adams, whom Pendleton knew to be a master at reading the room, rose and seconded his cousin's motion. Then both took their seats.

Pendleton drew in a thoughtful breath before rising from his chair. "Mr. President, and fellow delegates, it is true that there are those in this room who have experienced the results of serious indiscretions by our Motherland. We are in agreement that these must not be ignored."

He nodded to the Adamses. "To date, however, Britain's reckless actions have only had direct impact on the colonies to the north, New England if you will. Since the remainder of us are under the impression they already have a very capable commander, I see no reason to replace him with one from the South."

"With all due respect, Colonel Pendleton," the voice was that of John Adams, "it is only a matter of time before Britain's indiscretions, as you call them, will spill over into the Middle and Southern Colonies."

Pendleton paused before giving his reply. "Our hearts are with you and your colony, and we must stand united in defense of American liberty. However, if we proceed with the proposal from the Adamses, I am afraid the door to reconciliation will be forever closed." He raised one eyebrow, while trading a glance with Hancock. "If, on the other hand, we make no drastic changes while allowing our most recent petitions to be heard in London, Parliament and the king would be disposed to respond favorably."

"We have sought redress for a decade now," someone said. "It is past time for us to act."

"I believe the recent bloodshed will help London see things in a different light," Pendleton said, "causing them to consider the real cost of not granting our request." He nodded to the president, then sat down.

The war of words continued around him, some expressing support for Washington's appointment, and others standing with Pendleton against it. During a short recess, snippets of conversations made it clear the cousins from Massachusetts Bay were exercising their skills of persuasion.

Pendleton closed his eyes in prayer. When they opened, he knew what he must do. The colonies must show Britain a united front, even if it meant sacrificing his earlier stand. He must cast his vote with the others to make clear the colonies stood together in resistance against the unlawful acts of the Motherland. The men reconvened and voted unanimously in favor of Washington as their choice for general.

The day's adjournment finally came, and delegates scattered. As was his custom, Pendleton remained in his chair at the State House, deep in thought, before pushing himself to his feet and drifting to the window. He pulled back an edge of the dark covering, intended to keep the proceedings secret. Several men still mingled in the courtyard.

A rustle in the back startled him, and he turned to see Washington standing in the doorway.

"Colonel Pendleton," Washington said as he walked toward his fellow Virginian. "I am in need of your services."

"Anything I can do for you, my friend." Pendleton pushed back the sorrow welling up within him.

"If my country desires to bestow on me an honor to which I did not aspire, I must see to it that my family will be taken care of in case of my demise. I will need someone to draw up my Last Will and Testament to make sure my estate is handled according to my wishes."

Pendleton nodded. "I will be happy to assist you."

"Also, public speaking is not where I have placed my focus over the years." Washington grinned. "Yet I would like to be prepared, if called upon, to say a few words by way of acceptance. I would be most grateful for your assistance with that as well."

"Then we had better get busy," Pendleton said, extending one hand toward the door.

Pendleton returned the quill to its inkwell as he rubbed the soles of his shoes against the wooden-slat floor of the military tent. Could there be any more appropriate place on earth to write the new general's acceptance speech and Last Will and Testament? Pendleton handed the speech to Washington. "Take your time and see if this is to your liking."

The two men sat in silence for several minutes while the general read, then Washington picked up the pen and wrote a few words. "I've added a short phrase in the portion related to declining pay for my services."

Pendleton reviewed the change, then nodded. "Very appropriate."

The flap to the marquee tent flew open, and there stood Pendleton's tentmate.

"I'm so sorry, Uncle. I did not realize you were with someone. I can come back."

"Come." Pendleton stood and motioned for the young man to join them, then he turned to Washington. "General Washington, you remember my nephew, Jack Taylor. Neither of us could resist the opportunity for him to have a front row seat of the events this journey has afforded. Or to explore such faraway places as this."

The two men exchanged polite nods.

"I fear I have interrupted important business," Jack said.

Washington turned his focus back to Pendleton. "I believe we have completed our tasks here."

"We have." Pendleton picked up the general's Last Will and Testament and passed the document to Washington. "I know your time here is limited, but please send this to Mrs. Washington before leaving town."

Washington tucked the pages into his waistcoat pocket. "Thank you, my friend. Rest assured, it will happen." He stood and walked toward the tent's entrance, then paused and turned back to Pendleton. "Please keep me informed of any new developments with Lord Dunmore and of anyone who may be a wolf in sheep's clothing."

"I will. Perhaps this summer will determine whether we shall be slaves, or a wicked administration be sacrificed to our freedom."

Washington departed, and Pendleton secured the flap, then turned to his nephew.

"Lord Dunmore?" Jack cocked an eye half open at Pendleton. "Wolves in sheep's clothing?"

"News has arrived that Lord Dunmore took refuge aboard the Man of War, along with his family." Pendleton released a thin breath of air. "If evidence proves he is the one responsible for the injuries caused by the trap at the magazine's door in Williamsburg, he deserves to be assassinated."

Jack lifted an eyebrow. "I rarely hear such unfavorable words flow from your mouth."

"Intentional malice must be punished. As for the wolves, some suspect Richard Bland may not be as loyal to America as he makes himself out to be. He left here more than a month ago. I'd like to think it was simply to get back to business in Virginia, and not to flee the rumors swirling about him. It hurts me to say so, but I fear the rumors could have a just foundation. If so, he must be removed from his roles both here and at home, then cast into obscurity. The cause is much greater than any one man." The words tasted like vinegar spilling over his tongue.

Pendleton flipped one hand away from his body as if shooing away the unpleasantries. "Both my mind and constitution are ready for a break. Let's turn our attention to supper, shall we, before returning to the work at hand."

Jack walked toward the corner of the tent and picked up a few papers from his cot. "I simply came for this. I promised to meet with someone during supper." He walked to the door. "But, if you prefer, I can change my plans."

"No need," Pendleton said. "I could use some time to reflect. And since the military drills come even earlier than the rooster's crow back home, I wouldn't mind turning in soon."

Jack left, and Pendleton sank to the edge of his cot. Helping his fellow man brought a joy like no other, but some Last Wills and Testaments carried more potent reminders of death. His hand ran across the coarse military blanket covering his bed, his eyes squinting to a narrow gaze. General Washington had counted the cost.

Pendleton, too, would continue to fight against tyranny and protect the colonies, as well as future generations.

The colonists would prepare for war, but not accept it as certain. Not yet.

Not until no other option remained.

Pendleton was sworn to protect those who had sent him to Philadelphia. He must not let them down.

CHAPTER 13

Pomp and Ceremony

June 18 - July 30, 1775

The cool ale slid down Henry's throat as he stood and watched the river meander past the tavern, the breeze from a few days prior a distant memory. Delegates to Congress mingled about, doing their best to paint war in a positive light. The gathering provided an opportunity to send off the new general with all the fanfare he deserved.

"Mr. Henry." Benjamin Franklin's voice came from behind him.

Henry spun around and nodded in greeting, a bit of his drink spilling over his glass in the process. Ideological differences aside, the opportunity to get to know the colonies' most well-known diplomat and natural philosopher had been an unexpected gift. His stout frame, broad shoulders, and balding head added to his mythical qualities. "Ah, Dr. Franklin. I trust this occasion finds you well."

"It does," Franklin said. "And if you would allow me to mingle business with pleasure, somber as it may be, I have an idea to share with you."

"I would be pleased to hear it," Henry said.

"It pertains to one of the committees of which you are a member," Franklin said. "We have a lot to consider when dealing with the Indian Nations and do not want the king to have his wish of their taking up the hatchet against us."

Henry took another sip from his glass. "Securing and preserving their friendship could prove to be critical to our success."

Franklin shot Henry a sly grin. "Yes, and I believe I have devised a way for Congress to claim jurisdiction over the western territories."

Henry's eyes widened at the sight of the guest of honor approaching from behind Franklin.

Franklin continued. "Some of us have a vested interest—"

"Pardon me, gentlemen," Washington said. "I do not want to interrupt, but when convenient, I would appreciate a word with Mr. Henry."

Franklin swept his arm toward Henry, his lips curving into a grin. "By all means, General Washington. My matter can certainly wait." Franklin took two steps back. "Mr. Henry, let's also talk soon about the boundary dispute between our respective colonies. If we are able to add some brotherly love into the equation, I believe we can bring the matter to a happy conclusion." Franklin departed with a polite bow, and Washington turned to face Henry.

"General," Henry said, "let me congratulate you on your appointment."

Washington's eyes met Henry's gaze. "The honor is tempered with the fear that I am unequal to the station in which my country has placed me."

"I have admired you during our decade of serving together as burgesses," Henry said, "and am sure I will continue to do so."

"Remember, Mr. Henry, what I now tell you." Washington blinked back the tears. "From the day I enter upon the command of the American armies, I date my fall and the ruin of my reputation." Washington shook his head. "But since I have submitted to my country's request, I must be diligent in my preparations."

"Except in passing, I have seldom seen you since your acceptance a few days ago."

"I have been quite busy," Washington said. "Since the days to come are uncertain, I wanted to speak with you while I had the opportunity."

"Of course," Henry said.

"Mr. Henry, I have a number of questions for which I need answers from Congress." Washington shifted his weight. "They pertain to the number of subordinate officers, commissions, and allowances for aides-de-camp. I would like you to secure those answers for me."

"At your service."

"Good," Washington said. "Then, in the next day or two, I will put together a list of questions for you to submit to the delegates."

Henry grinned. "Perhaps Congress will grant me a military commission."

Washington's face tightened, and his lips rolled into a contained smile. "Perhaps. But for now, let's keep our focus on getting the answers we need." Washington took a step back and squared his posture. "Now, if you will excuse me."

A few days later, the pomp and ceremony of war unfolded before Henry in fine fashion. The sound of fifes and drums filled the air with patriotic tunes, sending his spirit soaring. He waved his arms above his head in rhythm with the beat. "Isn't this grand?" he shouted above the music.

He elbowed his way to the front of the crowd lining the street in front of Pennsylvania's State House. Washington stood tall in his newly-obtained blue regalia, complete with yellow buttons and gold epaulettes.

Surrounded by the boisterous crowd of well-wishers, he looked the part of a general heading off to fulfill his duties. Neighing came from the direction of Philadelphia's large light horse troop, each man outfitted in his dress uniform. Even children joined in by whirling their toy guns.

Washington's new aide-de-camp rushed to his side and offered a hand as the general placed his foot into the stirrup of one of his five new horses. Onlookers erupted into applause.

Seeing Thomas Jefferson's familiar face, Henry saddled up beside him and nudged his more subdued colleague, just arrived from Virginia. "If this doesn't get you excited, I don't know what will."

At Henry's encouragement, Jefferson yielded and put his hands together. "Not all of us are, dare I say, as theatrical as you. Perhaps Virginia's Convention chose me to replace Mr. Randolph because of the similarities he and I share."

"He is your kin, is he not?"

"Distant. On my mother's side." Jefferson grinned. "Maybe something is in our blood that tempers our more dramatic side."

"We were eager for your arrival," Henry said. "What kept you so long?"

Jefferson's Scottish complexion flushed a peachy glow. "We were lost, so it took a full ten days to get here."

"Lost?" Henry said.

Jefferson nodded, then grimaced at the jostling going on around him.

The beating of drums roared in the background. Henry bent closer to Jefferson's ear to be heard. "Well, if you need help finding your way around the city, I will be delighted to be of service."

"You may not know this," Jefferson said, "but I paid a brief visit to Philadelphia nine years ago."

"Really?"

"I came to get inoculated against smallpox."

Henry chuckled. "Both smallpox and the inoculation continue to be popular."

"Smallpox is common," Jefferson said, "but certainly not popular."

Many of the delegates, Massachusetts Bay first among them, scurried to the nearby carriages. Washington handed a letter to one of the servants. Though noise from the crowd muted the general's words, his lips made his request clear: "Send this to Mrs. Washington as soon as possible." The servant took the paper, then hurried away. Washington nodded at his four newly-appointed generals, then, with a swift kick, urged his horse into motion.

Henry surveyed the military leaders who would accompany General Washington to their respective appointments. If they could serve regardless of their military talent or experience, perhaps he could do the same back home.

"Ready for a stroll?" Henry asked.

"I will walk with the caravan for a while," Jefferson said, "but need to get back to acquiring the information I missed before my arrival."

"Never fear," Henry said. "I will be more than happy to convey to you whatever I can. Of course, the news received late yesterday from Boston will justify our recent movements toward war."

The parade rolled into motion like a flock of birds leaving for their winter homes, pulling Henry and Jefferson along with it.

"No one wants to believe that Joseph Warren was among the fallen."

"'Tis a deep loss," Henry said. "Yet we needed a breach on our affections to arouse the country to action."

Jefferson raised an eyebrow. "Perhaps."

"Bunker's Hill may serve as a rallying cry for moving forward," Henry said. "The shots fired and lives lost should help awaken those who have been slow to accept action as a reasonable option. Just before your arrival, Congress set forth its recommendation to the colonies regarding training militia, ages sixteen to fifty. We also suggested that each colony form a Committee of Safety to oversee such matters." Henry jumped to miss the heels of those in front of him.

"In many ways," Jefferson said, "I would prefer to be back home, where I could make more of an impact."

The words cut deep into Henry's soul. "With the coolheaded men who try to rule things in Congress, you may be right. But don't underestimate the pamphlet you produced last year explaining our rights. Several here have expressed their admiration for your keen intellect and elegant style."

The trace of a smile touched Jefferson's lips.

"Nonetheless," Henry said, "things will wind down here in a few weeks, then we can return home—where the action really is."

Henry put one foot into the stirrup and hoisted the other over his horse, casting a parting glimpse at Philadelphia. More than five weeks had passed since Washington's departure, and although it had been a grueling few months for many, Henry saw little activity thanks to Congress keeping him on the sidelines.

"Petitions, petitions, and more petitions," he mumbled. "And no real action." Henry's shoulders drooped. How could one more petition to the king, or even to the people of Great Britain, do any good? The time for talk had passed. Or should have. Preparing for war while negotiating for peace—

"Mr. Henry." The voice came from the direction of City Tavern.

Henry pulled his mount around to see John Adams hastening across the cobblestone street, Benjamin Franklin sauntering behind.

"Mr. Henry." Adams bent over and put both hands on his thighs, then held up his palm as he gasped for air.

"Take your time, Mr. Adams," Henry chuckled. "No need to have an apoplectic fit."

Adams drew in a few deep breaths. "Mr. Henry, we simply wanted to say goodbye."

Henry smiled down at his Massachusetts Bay friend. "It has been a pleasure getting to know you."

"I feel we share a kindred spirit." Adams stroked the mane of Henry's horse.

Henry nodded.

Franklin strolled up beside the two men. "Mr. Henry, I regret we were unable to settle the Indian affairs during this session. Maybe next time."

The clickety-clack of carriages rolled by in pace with the hustle and bustle of the big city.

"Gentlemen," Henry said, "I wonder if my services could be better utilized back home."

"In Virginia?" Franklin asked.

Henry leaned into his horse. "I agree with Mr. Adams. America is like a large fleet, in that the swiftest sailors must wait for the dullest and slowest. You may have noticed that I tire easily when tasked with waiting."

Adams nodded. "'Tis true."

"You gentlemen," Henry said, "have the patience of Job, which is to be commended. But I have grown restless."

A sly grin spread across Franklin's countenance. "And your plans for back home?"

"While Congress awaits a reply from the king regarding its so-called 'Olive Branch' petition," Henry said, "I believe it is time for me to prepare for military service, if my colony will have me. Though our colleagues claim we are not raising armies for the purpose of separating from the Motherland, it is foolish to pretend that is not the ultimate goal."

Franklin nodded. "If we make ourselves sheep, the wolves will eat us."

"At some point," Adams chimed in, "what we claim to be our *last* petition to the king will actually be so. With Congress' recent rejection of Lord North's plan for reconciliation, it may just be a matter of time."

Henry steadied his horse, impatiently pawing at the ground. "And, when that day comes, it is my earnest wish that many Virginians might see service. Earlier today, I wrote to General Washington these exact sentiments. I have also supplied him with answers to the questions he left with me before his departure."

"We would love to see you back here in September," Adams said, "but want you to be where you are needed most." Adams patted the horse's neck, then stepped back.

"If I do not return to Philadelphia," Henry said, "I will most certainly make use of the postal service, now led by none other than our esteemed Dr. Franklin."

Franklin grinned.

"I will count on it," Adams said.

"Farewell, gentlemen." Henry urged his horse into a gallop and rode away, left, once again, to his own thoughts. Yes, that many Virginians would see service. His colony's troops would need a leader, and if the offer came, he was ready to accept. After all, Lord Dunmore had run scared after Henry threatened to march on Williamsburg. Virginia needed their favorite son to step up and finish the job he had begun. Then, with Pendleton certain to be reelected to Congress, Henry would have free rein at home.

CHAPTER 14

Shuffling the Deck

AUGUST - SEPTEMBER 1775

A bead of sweat trickled down Pendleton's back. His friend Lieutenant William Woodford stood by his side during a pause in his duties. On the meadow spread out before them, soldiers stood in formation before the more junior officers. Pendleton's lips pulled into a smile. Home. Even the military tent in which he and Jack had lodged while in Philadelphia, now set up behind him, seemed more at ease on Virginia's plains. Pennsylvania could keep her big city, especially the demerits of some of its inhabitants. His county's "big city," Bowling Green, Virginia, soothed not only his body but his very soul.

The rhythmic beating of the military drum pulled Pendleton's attention back to the military exercises unfolding before him and the fifteen hundred spectators. Officers barked orders to their troops.

"No tyranny!" someone shouted from the crowd.

Muskets fired, producing plumes of smoke.

Pendleton squeezed his hand into a ball as he pulled it to his mouth, covering the cough threatening to escape. He shot Woodford a sheepish grin. "I'll be fine," he said as he pulled out his handkerchief.

Woodford wagged his head. "Maybe I should continue as your second so you can go home and let your wife nurse you back to health. I'm happy to continue to fill in for you at the convention and could keep you abreast of any important happenings."

"No," Pendleton said. "You said yourself they are floundering without its usual leadership. I plan to be in Richmond tomorrow, along with the others who have returned from Philadelphia." He turned to cough into his kerchief. His eyes winced shut as he choked back the thought of leaving the convention while in such need. "Besides, with Wronghead tucked away on the Man of War, we must make use of our advantage."

Woodford snorted a laugh. "Lord Dunmore has no plans to return to us, but additional troops and warships are said to be on their way to our colony."

"Another reason we must waste no time preparing." Pendleton narrowed his eyes into a squint. "With no definite response from England regarding the battles at Lexington and Bunker's Hill, we must continue to trust the loose reports which favor the prospect of peace while readying ourselves for whatever may come. Once the Motherland hears of the colonists' preparations to defend themselves, perhaps she will abandon any thought of taking up arms against her own."

"If you will excuse me for a moment," Woodford said, one palm uplifted toward Pendleton.

One of the young men from the field had marched to within a few feet of the two men, then halted. A few words with Woodford, then he returned to his comrades, leaving the men to their conversation.

"All is well?" Pendleton asked.

Woodford gave a clipped nod.

Against his body's will, Pendleton pushed his shoulders back to their proper position. His chest complained, but he remained resolute.

Additional matters demanded attention. "It seems I sent the military tent, flag, and drum just in time."

"Yes, your gifts are much appreciated. And once someone can be found to play the fifes . . ." Woodford kicked at the dirt beneath his feet. "I am afraid I have additional news. But with your current condition . . ."

Pendleton levied a piercing glare toward Woodford. "Whatever it is that ails me is secondary to protecting our fellowman. Let me hear it."

An awkward silence settled between them before Woodford continued. "You know that Congress decided that Virginia, along with Pennsylvania and Maryland, should raise troops. Virginia's Convention has decided on three regiments, each with a commander and one to be over them all."

"Yes." Pendleton squinted.

"Well, three days ago, the convention appointed those men."

The drills playing out before Pendleton faded as he began to question his own preconceptions. He furrowed his brow, then tilted his head toward Woodford.

"I was placed over the Third Regiment."

"The Third?" Pendleton said. "As the commander of all Virginia's troops, you should be placed over its First Regiment."

Woodford eyes fixed on the ground beneath him. "The convention gave that honor to someone else."

The bands tightened across Pendleton's chest. "Who? Hugh Mercer, I hope."

"Patrick Henry."

"What?" Pendleton stared straight ahead but saw nothing, struggling to make sense of it all. The cadence from the drum pounded inside his head. "He has absolutely no military experience. But you"—he turned to face his protégé—"you served us well in the war against the French and Indians. Under Colonel Washington, no less. Not to mention you are a third-generation professional soldier."

"I know," Woodford said. "Since Mr. Henry had not yet returned from Philadelphia, his friends did a lot of politicking on his behalf and ultimately pulled him through. He was placed over the First Regiment and made commander in chief of all our troops."

"A man's experience and ability to lead the troops with wisdom, not popularity, should have been the guiding light. Courage lies in the heart of the man who is willing to say so. It's clear that I should have been here to help illuminate the path, rather than in Philadelphia."

"Others did argue based on Mr. Henry being a stranger to the art of war, but I'm afraid it is already settled," Woodford said. "Mr. Henry will command the First Regiment and Thomas Nelson the Second."

"Perhaps I should stay in Virginia where I can help you and Colonel Nelson to pilot the less experienced Mr. Henry."

"I do have some good news," Woodford said.

"Please." The gruffness in his voice betrayed Pendleton's growing frustration.

"The previous convention adjourned without expelling Mr. Bland."

"They do not believe he is a traitor?"

Woodford shrugged. "I don't know if he is completely beyond suspicion, but we did not find enough evidence to prove his guilt."

A glimmer of hope. "He and Speaker Randolph are the only ones who have served as a burgess longer than I."

"With Mr. Randolph's poor health and Mr. Bland's advanced age, I believe the convention is counting on your leadership. I have no doubt they will vote to place you in a position of leadership soon."

Pendleton managed a weak smile, then suppressed another cough. "By God's grace, I will not let them down."

Click, click, click.

Henry's shoes hit against the floorboards as he followed Thomas Jefferson, Richard Henry Lee, Benjamin Harrison, and the ballot box down the church aisle to the privacy of the meeting room. Convention delegates sat in the same pews in Richmond where, five months before, Henry won many over with his passionate speech. The body's newly-elected president, Robert C. Nicholas, sat in place of the fatigued Randolph, who needed a bit of a reprieve from his duties before heading back to Philadelphia.

Despite the ups and downs of the previous few days, Henry's spirit continued to rejoice from the news he had received upon his arrival in Virginia. His desire for a military command had been granted. Murmurings that he was unfit to lead the troops, unacquainted with the art of war, and held no knowledge of military discipline only strengthened his resolve to prove them wrong. He would show them by living up to the trust the convention had placed in him when they elected him to its highest military post.

A win.

Too, his good friend George Mason, had slipped into Washington's empty seat as a delegate from Fairfax County. Another victory.

Muted conversations of the men whose heels he followed floated past Henry like a vapor as he continued to evaluate each side of the scale.

Securing gunpowder rounded out Henry's list of successes. While journeying back from Philadelphia, he had purchased one ton of it using the money received during his march to Williamsburg in May. The powder now sat in Baltimore. After much debate, the convention decided to have it transported to Virginia, leaving it up to Congress' new delegates to determine what to do with it.

On the loss side, the newly-elected delegates to Congress had not worked out according to Henry's hopes. A shuffling resulted in Woodford's move to colonel of Virginia's Second Regiment. And Pendleton *should* have been among those chosen to return to Philadelphia, leaving Henry with less to constrain him at home. Pendleton, however, had excused himself from nomination, in his ever-graceful way, due to his declining state of health. He would remain in Virginia. But what role would he play?

Beneath his jacket, Henry rubbed one side of his knotted stomach. Ballots in the box that Jefferson carried would elect members to the Committee of Safety—the committee that Henry helped create. That committee would oversee military affairs in Virginia in the coming months and have overarching control over Henry and his troops.

Thud. The ballot box now sat on the table in front of them. Jefferson, Henry, and the other two assigned to tally the results each pulled out a chair. Henry's attention returned to the task at hand.

"Gentlemen, are you ready to proceed?" Jefferson asked.

Henry pulled in a lungful of air, nodded, then pasted on a smile.

With each member of the convention allowed to nominate several men, nearly a thousand names waited to be counted. Reviewing the first few dozen ballots made it clear. Pendleton would be on the committee. No surprise there.

Jefferson read aloud the remaining ballots. "George Mason. Edmund Pendleton. Richard Bland." He paused after each name to allow the others time to verify, then record, the information.

The candidate with the most votes would almost certainly become the committee's leader. Henry couldn't bring himself to eye the page containing the results. Of the fifty or so names on the list, less than twenty claimed a significant number of votes. Only eleven would sit on the committee, and George Mason and Edmund Pendleton appeared to have the most.

Richard Henry Lee read aloud as he tallied votes for each nominee. "For George Mason, one, two, three . . ."

Henry tapped his foot against the floorboards as the moments passed.

"Seventy-one, seventy-two," Lee said. "Seventy-two votes for George Mason."

Good news. Yet Henry's stomach churned. His eyes refused to look at the ticks beside Pendleton's name as Lee read them off.

"Sixty-nine," Lee said. "Seventy, seventy-one."

Henry closed his eyes.

"Seventy-two, seventy-three, seventy-four," Lee continued. "Seventy-five, seventy-six, seventy-seven. Seventy-seven votes for Edmund Pendleton."

Henry's eyelids lifted.

"Well, that's it, gentlemen." Jefferson pushed back from the table. "I think I will stand for the recount." He scanned the faces of the other three men. "Mr. Henry, are you all right?"

"Yes," Henry nodded. Apart from the feeling that someone had just punched him in the gut, he was fine.

The recount confirmed the results, and the men returned to the sanctuary to present them to the other delegates.

Nine days in Virginia had provided Henry with more activity than an entire summer in Philadelphia. And with Dunmore's recent threats to attack Williamsburg and bombard Norfolk, Henry would show Pendleton and Woodford that he could do the job. He was sure of it.

The pungent scent of freshly-harvested tobacco leaves greeted Pendleton upon his arrival in Hanover Town. A few weeks at home after the convention had supplied him with enough strength to travel the thirty miles to fulfill his duty. He stood at a small table inside one of the local taverns, floor swept clean. With only two members of the

Committee of Safety absent, eight sat before him in the semicircle of chairs. During his month of leading them, many had shared their common concerns.

Several men stood to the side, at attention, each ready to carry out his commission as one of Virginia's military officers. Pendleton scanned their faces. No doubt, they were sincere in what they had sworn to do: to be "faithful and true to the colony and dominion of Virginia" and to defend "the just rights of America."

Pendleton dragged up a smile and held out the parchment to Patrick Henry, the man standing before him. "Mr. Henry, as commander in chief of all forces to be raised for the protection and defense of this colony, we expect you to execute these duties to the best of your abilities." The words sliding from his mouth were wrought with concern. Would Henry's best be enough to protect those he might lead into battle?

The two things which held Pendleton back from an all-out effort to prevent Henry's commission scampered through his mind. First, as the president of the committee which oversaw Viginia's military affairs, Pendleton could keep a close eye on him. Second, Henry would be obligated to disband his troops upon orders from the convention and serve at its pleasure. And no longer. The Committee of Safety made their expectations of Henry clear: He would "pay due obedience to all orders and instructions . . . from the convention or Committee of Safety."

Faces of Pendleton's loved ones flooded his mind's eye—Jack, Edmund Jr., John Penn, and so many others he held dear. He would not allow Henry's inexperience to result in the death of Virginia's own. Not now. Not ever.

Pendleton would find out soon enough if Henry's lack of military experience would require intervention. Perhaps Pendleton's health had returned just in time for the challenging days that lay ahead.

In the meantime, Pendleton and his committee would wrestle through how to best raise the needed regulars and, perhaps more challenging, obtain the necessary supplies. But would all the kettles, canteens, drums, and fifes be enough to overcome the inexperience of Virginia's new commander in chief? Would good men be placed in harm's way due to Henry's lack of military knowledge and understanding?

With Henry's commissioning a few days behind him, the road leading to Williamsburg came to life. And to his amazement, he was at the center of it. The volunteers who had spent their summer watching over the capital surrounded him with shouts of joy.

"Our leader has arrived!"

"Colonel Henry will lead us to victory!"

"Huzzah!"

Henry wagged his head. The confidence which Virginia's Convention and Committee of Safety continued to deny him flowed generously from his troops.

The few soldiers carrying arms lifted them skyward, while others danced in the street. A grin crossed Henry's face, spreading so wide it hurt. After a handful of salutes from the men, they ushered him around to the other end of the troops.

"Lead the way!" one of them bellowed.

Henry's spirit soared.

He spun around and, with his back to the men, motioned for them to follow. "To our new encampment, men. To the broad plain just beyond the college." Henry's arms swung upward to the rhythm of his own heart, and the men cheered as they fell in line.

Life was good.

A few days later, Henry stood at the edge of the military camp, his nose wrinkling at the stench. Smoke from the cooking fires, sporadic as it was, lessened odors from the excrement, and the early fall weather provided a bit of relief. At word of Henry's appointment, the field on the back side of the college had begun to fill with troops. Yet junior officers had failed at implementing Henry's orders about cleanliness, discipline, and other items critical to forming an army. If left unattended, illness, lice, and any number of other maladies might cripple an otherwise powerful force.

Logistical headaches permeated Henry's new role. Reminders for soldiers to stay in camp, rather than meander into town, became routine. The meaning of various drumbeats must be taught, and reports about the state of their equipment were difficult to obtain. In addition to three hours spent in learning the discipline of woods fighting, the companies were to spend an hour each day in drills.

Henry's gaze moved from one group of men to the next. Provisions had trickled in, yet some remained without a tent for sleeping, while others used a rug rather than a blanket for warmth. And not all muskets the men had brought from home were in good working order.

A light breeze brushed Henry's face, then the flutter of a flag caught his eye. The corners of his mouth turned upward. A personalized version of a banner from South Carolina flew high above one group of soldiers. In addition to the image of a coiled rattlesnake and "Don't Tread on Me," the words "The Culpeper Minutemen" fanned across the top of the flag, along with Henry's words from earlier in the year, "Liberty or Death." Henry's battle cry also graced the front of the men's green hunting shirts.

Henry dipped his head toward the group. He had inspired the men from Culpeper County and, in turn, they had inspired him. Everything about them—their rifles, scalping knives and tomahawks in their belts, and buck-tailed hats on their heads—assured Henry that they were ready.

CHAPTER 15

John Penn Goes to Philly

EARLY OCTOBER – EARLY NOVEMBER 1775

The autumn air cooled John Penn's face as the rocking chair found its rhythm on his cousin's front porch. His horse, tied to the post at the foot of the stairs, awaited final preparations. Were Penn's morning aches and pains a result of the many miles traveled or from the strains that threated to push him and his mentor even further apart?

Varying hues of ruby and gold from Edmundsbury's maple trees dotted the landscape, the dew sparkling beneath the morning sun. Beyond the house, slaves milled about the plantation with their early-morning chores. Methodical creaks from the rocker took him back to heartwarming images of playing in the yard as a child more than two decades past. Then, as he grew into a young man, he enjoyed pleasant evenings with the Pendletons as fireflies lit up the evening sky while crickets and frogs composed their own type of symphony. In recent years, almost nothing, yet everything, had changed.

"Mista Penn." The woman's voice blended with childhood memories yet pulled Penn back from his meandering.

He smiled up at the servant woman, then lifted his hands to receive the mug being handed to him. "Thank you, Cloe."

"You wasn't here for a minute, was ya?"

"No, I wasn't." Penn grinned. "There've been some good memories on this porch, haven't there?"

"Yass, suh. Sure have."

Penn wrapped his hands around the warm mug, drawing in a lungful of the chocolatey aroma floating from it. "And this morning's breakfast was as good as I remember. If anything, you've made it even better."

Cloe's face broke into a smile, crooked teeth and all. "Colonel Pendleton said he—"

The front door swung open and Pendleton stepped out.

"Ah, there he be," Cloe said. "If you men will 'scuse me, I got things ta tend to."

Pendleton cast a knowing look at Penn. "Cloe never did like goodbyes, did she?"

Penn mumbled an affirmation, then took a sip from his mug, not yet ready to make eye contact. His late arrival the night before left little time for broaching the more sensitive subjects. With many miles between him and Congress, he could not linger nor wait for a better time. He shifted in his chair. "I received word that William and James are among those who marched from Culpeper to Williamsburg."

"My nephews?" The lines etched deep across Pendleton's face.

Penn nodded.

"William is young enough to face the challenge of the uncertainties that lie ahead. But James must be nearing forty years of age." Pendleton cleared his throat. "Just because Congress set fifty as the upper age for enlistment doesn't mean I have to like it."

Penn took another sip, the warmth of the beverage calming the turmoil rising within him. The pain reflected in his cousin's eyes at the thought of loved-ones placed in harm's way gave Penn pause. The cost of war had become more real. Was it worth the price? Ready to share another tidbit, he launched back in. "I believe Nathaniel's son Henry volunteered to be a minuteman."

"And I heard Nathaniel Jr. left to join General Washington in Boston," Pendleton said.

The front door swung open once again, and Penn's body servant stepped out, lugging one of Penn's travel bags. He gave a clipped nod to the two men, scooted down the steps, then went about his work.

Pendleton walked over to a free rocking chair and took a seat. "Enough of what is going on with our kinfolk. What can you tell me about July's armed rebellion in North Carolina?"

Penn set his empty mug on floorboards beside him. "The North Carolina governor blames our Committees of Safety for the burning of Fort Johnston."

"No surprise." Pendleton let out a scoffing laugh, then pushed with his feet to get his chair to rocking. "With both of our governors in hiding, the committees will be the ones to receive any pent-up criticism."

"We are working hard to raise the two regiments and minutemen that Congress requested of us. We have also been busy collecting corn and other necessary supplies to send to Massachusetts."

"Good," Pendleton said, bringing his chair to a standstill. "I can only imagine how difficult it must be for them to have a blockaded port. They need all the prayers and supplies we can provide."

Penn's eyes followed the movement of his body servant busy preparing the horses, snorting at the fuss around them.

Pendleton strummed his fingers on the armrest of his rocking chair. "What is the general sense of things in North Carolina—that of the everyday citizen?"

"Those in Mecklenburg County have signed a document." Penn forced the words from his mouth, not wishing to share the news with his cousin. "A document that declares they are a free and independent people who are only under the control of God and Congress."

Pendleton groaned, then hoisted himself to his feet. "We should always be under the Lord's control, but to declare we are independent from British authority is premature. To be sure, the Motherland has made serious blunders in recent days, but until she makes clear that redress is impossible, that is what we should seek." He ambled over to the front of the porch, and rested one hand on its railing.

The words in Penn's throat struggled to push through. "I do believe many in my colony still pledge allegiance to the Crown." He swallowed the news that North Carolina's Congress had placed him on a committee designed to help change their minds. "In fact, North Carolina's Provincial Congress rejected Dr. Franklin's proposal for a colonial confederation. We did, however, vote to move toward purchasing arms and ammunition."

"In short supply," Pendleton said, "if money is even available to procure them. Nevertheless, we need to prepare as best we can, lest we are unable to settle things without the use of arms. And, as neighboring colonies, we need to be ready to help each other."

"We will be there for you, if called upon."

"These are tough times." Pendleton pivoted to face Penn. "And, it is no secret, I am concerned for our family who will be in harm's way. They are in my thoughts and prayers throughout the day. May God grant us reconciliation with our Motherland and, if it does not come, the internal peace that only He can provide during times of great trial."

Penn stood and walked over to his cousin. "The North Carolina Congress produced a document pledging allegiance to the king. I was among those who signed it."

Pendleton's eyes opened wide. "*You* signed it?"

"I know it may not seem consistent with my past behavior, but the one pence I refused to pay last year for my treasonous remarks against the king was personal. The statement I signed several weeks ago was on behalf of those in my colony whom I represent."

Penn's body servant patted the horse's rump, then turned to face the porch. "Mista Penn, the horse is ready at your convenience."

Penn tucked his chin in acknowledgement.

"I have missed you, John." Pendleton placed a hand on Penn's shoulder. "Various things compete for our loyalties, and I wish times were not as complex as they are."

"Thank you," Penn whispered as he gripped Pendleton's forearm. "I have missed the simplicity of days gone by." Penn's lips eased into a smile. "At least there was more family on the other end of my fleeing—uh, moving—to North Carolina. It has been good to be near them. I do miss Mother. Next month will be a year since . . ."

Pendleton's arms opened wide and drew Penn close. "With my own mother but five years in the grave, the pain of losing those dearest to you is still fresh on my heart too."

Penn softened in the kindness of his cousin's embrace, then Pendleton pushed him to arm's length, his eyes glimmering with unshed tears.

Pendleton released his protégé. "Missing them reveals the preciousness of the relationships we have lost. But remember, for those of us who have an eternal hope in the One who made us, the loss is but temporary. We will see your dear mother again. And mine."

Penn nodded. "I must go. Many miles lie between me and Philadelphia." Penn gripped his cousin's forearm once again, released, then took a few steps down the stairs.

"Your North Carolina colleagues must think very highly of you to give you this honor," Pendleton said. "When you arrive in Philadelphia, please give everyone my best. Especially those delegates from Virginia."

"I will. Thank you for your hospitality." Penn hoisted himself onto his mount, then cast his gaze back to his cousin. "And thank you for the good information you've given me about Philadelphia. I am certain it will give me a great advantage as I learn my way around."

His squeezed his legs into his mount, leaned forward, then he was off to the adventures that lie before him.

Penn shifted his weight from one leg to another, then took another drink from his mug, careful to stay clear of attendants whisking by with plates of food. City Tavern was all that Pendleton said it would be —gracious dining and buzzing with the latest political maneuverings. All around him, chatter rose up from delegates seated at tables, both large and small. Others meandered in and out of the large dining room, seeming to carry on multiple conversations at once. Getting his bearings was proving to be—

"Mr. Penn?"

Penn spun around, careful not to spill any of his drink. Two gentlemen hurried toward him, one rather stout, his white wig and lace cuffs accentuating his velvety brown overcoat. The other stood tall and refined, his ruddy cheeks emitting a welcoming glow.

"'Tis I," Penn said.

"We received word from Colonel Pendleton that you would be arriving soon," the stout man said. "Allow us to introduce ourselves. I am Peyton Randolph, and this is my fellow Virginian Thomas Jefferson."

Penn straightened and bowed his head in greeting. "What a pleasure."

"The pleasure is ours," Randolph said, looking the part his pedigree afforded him.

"My cousin speaks highly of you, especially of your abilities to forge compromise between his conservative faction and those bent on more radical ways," Penn said with a twinkle in his eye. "Say, those such as Patrick Henry and Richard Henry Lee."

Randolph's eyebrows curled down, yet his lips hinted at a smile. "Your cousin's kindhearted spirit has made working with him a pleasure these many years, and my entire household enjoys having him in our home."

Jefferson perked up. "Mr. Randolph's reputation preceded him here. Those in various colonies already knew of his abilities to lead with grace and dignity before they elected him to lead the first Congress."

"We each have our role to play," Randolph said.

"Yes," Jefferson said, "but some believe you may carry more on your shoulders than any one man should bear. Wrangling with King George and managing an undeclared war is not for the faint of heart."

Randolph shook his head. "I would hardly refer to my style as wrangling."

"True." Jefferson chuckled, then extended his arm toward an available table. "Shall we take a seat and continue our conversation?"

"There is nothing I would enjoy more," Randolph said. "But other matters require my attention this evening." He turned to Penn. "I will leave you with Colonel Jefferson who will orient you to what has transpired prior to your arrival. Good day, gentlemen." And with that, Randolph wobbled away.

"How thoughtful for him to take time to introduce himself," Penn said.

Jefferson nodded. "He cares for so many and so much. The New Englanders knew that electing such a Virginian to lead us would set the minds of many delegates at ease. Of course, it is John Hancock who leads us now. But enough of that. Shall we take advantage of the fine fare offered to us here?"

The two gentlemen ambled over to a table. Once settled, Penn wasted no time addressing the business at hand. "I apologize for my late arrival, but my election happened only after North Carolina chose my predecessor to be our colony's treasurer. He could not do both, thus they selected me to fill his role as a delegate. I am anxious to learn what I have missed so I can be ready to participate in whatever manner needed."

Jefferson smiled. "I can see Colonel Pendleton in you."

"I owe everything to him," Penn said.

"I am sure you will make him proud," Jefferson said. "Unfortunately, very little information needs to be conveyed. The Georgia colony is now represented. In the few weeks you have missed, we sent a committee to Cambridge, across the river from Boston, to meet with General Washington. We also began the initial steps of forming a navy."

"Is there not more to do?"

Jefferson shifted in his chair. "Until we receive a reply from the king regarding the petition we sent in May, there is little more we can do. The longer it takes to get a reply, the more the winds seem to shift toward war. So, we wait for news from London. I'm sure we will hear as soon as it arrives."

Penn adjusted the black band around his left arm, careful not to bump those standing nearby. The commencement of a month of mourning was not what he had envisioned for his opening days in the City of Brotherly Love. If only he could be the one to convey the news to Pendleton concerning the death of his longtime friend. Who would have imagined that the building where Peyton Randolph called the first Congress to order thirteen months before would now help usher him into eternity? A mere two weeks after Penn's arrival.

With the state funeral behind them, delegates began leaving the building. Carpenters' Hall still echoed the sounds of death amid the muted chatter of the mourners who remained. Two gentlemen emerged, gentlemen Penn recognized as Samuel and John Adams, and walked toward him.

"Mr. Penn?" Samuel Adams said in a hushed tone.

"Yes." Penn said. "I am he."

The man in the reddish-brown suit placed a hand upon his chest. "Samuel Adams at your service and my cousin, John," he said with a wave of his hand.

"Delighted," Penn said. "I had hoped to make your acquaintance." He dipped his head to where Reverend Duché had stood to conduct the service. "But not under these circumstances."

John Adams lifted one eyebrow. "A sad occasion, indeed. My cousin and I were just discussing the timing of Mr. Randolph's death." He traded a glance with Samuel, then turned his attention back to Penn. "You see, there was another colleague, a fellow Bostonian, who died on the exact same date last year. William Molineux was a true patriot." He looked down. "Even before I came around."

"Mr. Molineux," Samuel said, "died under suspicious circumstances. Some claim he died by an apoplectic fit, same as Mr. Randolph, but my cousin and I know better."

"Oh?" Penn said.

"He was a strong advocate for the patriotic cause," John said, "and had unique abilities, shall we say, to rally a crowd."

Samuel ducked his chin in agreement. "The British soldiers stationed within sight of his front door did not care for him, and I believe they are the ones who saw to it that his voice was silenced."

"Interesting," Penn said. "It seems we must stay vigilant or a common fate may befall us."

John flipped both palms upward and shrugged. "The arrest of Benjamin Church should send a signal to others who are considering working for the enemy."

"A reply from the king," Samuel said, "would certainly help our cause. Until then, it is more difficult to push forward with plans for war."

"There are a lot of things," John said, "that will need to be sorted out. Things that have kept my mind occupied."

"I would love to hear about them," Penn said.

"In due time, Mr. Penn," John said. "In due time."

Penn pushed his chair back from the makeshift desk in the State House meeting room. Other delegates milled about, each processing the news just arrived from London in his own way.

The king had refused to even receive the petition Congress had sent. No answer would be given. He simply trampled the olive branch under foot. Congress' efforts to help the colonies prepare for war would intensify. Penn's heart raced. Had the time arrived for speculation to give way to well-defined actions?

Penn's gaze inched around the room. With whom should he consult? His North Carolina colleagues stood near the table they shared, but he would save that battle for another day. He continued to survey his options. The Adams cousins. They would do. Penn stood and meandered around the other delegates until he stood before them.

"Gentlemen," Penn said, "could I have a word with you?"

Samuel furrowed his brow. "I would love nothing more, but there are others I must secure before they leave the building." Samuel looked at his cousin. "John?"

"I will be happy to speak with you, Mr. Penn," John said.

Samuel began to walk away, then turned back to the two men. "Rest assured that the actions of the king and his ministers will produce the grandest revolutions the world has ever seen."

Penn forced a lifeless smile. *Revolution.* Surely, many eyes would turn to Virginia for guidance. How would Pendleton and his colleagues respond to all that would be laid at their feet in the days ahead?

CHAPTER 16

Mr. Henry

November 1775

Henry watched as Colonel Woodford's Second Regiment marched out of Williamsburg toward Norfolk. The early November chill did little to temper the fiery sting resulting from recent communications from the Committee of Safety. Despite a month worth of efforts by Henry to ready his troops, the committee left little doubt as to what it thought of him: He was not up to handling the most important military challenge Virginia had faced since the conflict with the Motherland began. That assignment would be given to Pendleton's protégé, Colonel Woodford.

Henry's nostrils flared. The committee's request for him and his men to guard Williamsburg had been little more than a thinly veiled resolve to keep him out of the way. Guard Williamsburg? Dunmore's focus was on Norfolk, possibly to secure it as a new base of operations. Rumors indicated Dunmore had armed runaway slaves and that frigates would soon arrive from Boston to help reinforce his stance just off the coast. Had Williamsburg been in danger, Virginia's Convention and Committee of Safety would have stayed in Richmond to carry on its business rather than return to the capital. Pendleton's committee went so far as to loan Henry's Culpeper battalion of minutemen to Woodford for the expedition against Norfolk.

Had Henry's two main allies on the committee not taken ill, would they have been able to fight for a different outcome?

Drums, fifes, and colors—gifts from none other than Pendleton himself—paraded past Henry in a blur. He adjusted the black crepe wrapped around his arm, then his eyes went to the crepes on the arms of his officers passing before him. Randolph's death not only meant the personal bridge between Henry's and Pendleton's factions had been removed, but that Pendleton might take Randolph's place as leader of the convention. Just one more way Pendleton would be able to keep Henry right where he wanted him. Away from the action.

Then there were the notes. Notes in which Pendleton addressed Henry not as colonel, but as sir. To Henry, the commander in chief of Virginia's forces, the slight was apparent. In a more recent communique from the committee, they mentioned his title, yet the address remained as "sir." The notice itself openly questioned Henry's judgment for not attending certain meetings.

As things began to intensify, would Henry and his men be called upon to get involved in the action? He shifted his weight from one leg to the other. While waiting, he would demonstrate the same regard and respect he admonished his officers to show toward their counterparts.

Pendleton stood beside the bed, thankful for the accommodations that the Randoph home had provided through the years. Although his longtime friend and colleague was dead, Peyton Randolph's widow and servants continued to welcome Pendleton into their home. The dressing table, complete with mirror and chair, always made his stay a comfortable one. A small desk situated near the hearth provided a spot for late-night tasks. Yet now, the scent of death hovered near.

November's muted sun filtered through the second-story window of the Williamsburg home. Pendleton's two and a half months in Virginia had worn him to the bone. Managing Henry, Woodford, and his committee, while keeping Virginia's delegates to Congress informed of all the happenings, afforded scanty time for food and sleep. Former labors in various public employments, now appeared as recreation compared with the present. While Virginia's capital had been his second home for more years than he cared to count, he longed for his Caroline County forest.

He pushed the bedcurtain further out of the way. The newspaper lying on the bed beside the leather portmanteau demanded one last look. He slid onto the edge of the bed, picked up the paper, and ran his fingers across a piece he had read again and again. By the time he returned to Williamsburg, news of Virginia's resistance would have reached the king. Would it be enough to convince him that his colonies merely sought to defend their God-given rights, not to embrace a state of rebellion? The paper provided a glimmer of hope that it would. And with good news regarding the campaign in Canada and reports that Lord Dunmore would be recalled any day . . . . Pendleton folded the paper and placed it into his bag.

While the committee had been able to contain Henry's influence, the battle with Dunmore only seemed to intensify. Military supplies had been difficult to obtain but finally found their way into the hands of Woodford's troops, now making their way to Norfolk where Dunmore's formidable fleet sat well equipped to take on whatever came his way. Pendleton pinched the bridge of his nose. Then there was the censoring of potentially dangerous mail in order to help prevent desertions by troops. The lack of salt, Lord Dunmore's seizure of Norfolk's printing press, and the threat of armed runaway slaves added to Pendleton's concerns. Fortunately, the governor's attempt to use slaves as pawns only served to bring the people of Virginia together for the common cause.

Nevertheless, Norfolk's non-Tory population had fled for safer ground despite Pendleton's attempt to reassure them Virginia troops had been sent there for good, not harm. With so many strangers coming inland, additional precautions would be needed to guard against extreme Loyalists attempting to fit in, yet with an evil intent. Protecting those Pendleton had served for so many years stayed at his core. To them he would remain true. Yet his Majesty's actions in recent years provided the conservatives with more limited arguments against the radical's desired response, and signs pointed to a coming crossroads.

A light rap came at the door. "Colonel Pendleton?"

"Yes?" Pendleton's stomach knotted. Potential messages that would prevent his departure—

"We've got your horse ready."

A sense of relief flowed though Pendleton's body. "Thank you, Nero. I will be ready shortly."

"Yass, suh."

Pendleton stood and drifted to the window for one last look into the garden, murmurings of Henry's friends echoed in his mind. The decision to send Woodford, rather than Henry, was never a question for Pendleton. Randolph would have agreed. *Lord, why did you take him from us?* Henry did not have the military experience, nor the temperament, to be put in such a precarious situation as Norfolk currently afforded. This was not about popularity. Lives were at stake, and the committee would be faithful to the task the convention had entrusted to them.

With well-armed men now stationed at three strategic posts—Williamsburg, Hampton, and Norfolk—the committee could savor the much-needed reprieve. His family and own bed would be welcome sights for his weary body and soul. If a few men from Culpeper County could prevent Dunmore's men from coming ashore, then Woodford, to whom the committee had given broad authority, and his seven hundred troops should be able to keep the threat at bay. With Henry tucked away in Williamsburg for the winter, Pendleton could return home with a sense of tranquility.

Henry grabbed the teetering inkwell before any more liquid could spill onto the desk inside his recently-obtained winter quarters. Perhaps his return of the quill had been too forceful, yet finally taking action filled him with satisfaction. How dare the royal governor impose martial law and offer to free any slave who would take up arms on behalf of the Crown. Had the Committee of Safety's recess been what prompted Dunmore's threats against the people of Virginia? With the governor's landing and his men now marching toward Great Bridge, no one could expect Henry, as Virginia's commander in chief, to sit idly by. Did even Dunmore lack faith in Henry's military abilities?

The sooner Mr. Purdie received Henry's handwritten notice, the sooner he could make it into a broadside for distribution to all the county lieutenants. Time was of the essence.

He glanced around for something to wipe up the mess. The handkerchief lying atop a nearby pile would do. He snatched it up, spit into it, then rubbed the blob of ink threatening to roll over the side of the desk. Sliding the chair back from the desk while attempting to remain seated produced nothing but a noisy commotion. The vibrations shifted from the chair leg to Henry's own. *Ugh.* He dumped himself back into the seat, then wiped his hands on his breeches. A quick review of the note revealed it had not captured any stray ink. No need to rewrite his reply to Dunmore's venomous words of blackmail.

Once arrangements were made to alert the county lieutenants, Henry would ready his men while awaiting word from Pendleton or Woodford, the latter of whom had not even provided Henry with brief notes of correspondence. The committee would be back soon due to the new threat. But soon might be too late.

He stood, swiped up the notice, and reviewed his comments about Dunmore's proclamation being fatal to the public, forcing Henry to call for necessary patrols. He secured the document under his coat, then rushed down the stairs and out the door to Mr. Purdie's printshop. Success with this task would surely prompt the Committee of Safety to provide Henry with additional responsibilities. If not, Henry could take his complaints to the convention where Robert C. Nicholas, rather than Pendleton, had secured the role of president. Without the presidential gavel in his hand, Pendleton would not be able to stand in his way.

CHAPTER 17

𝕾𝖍𝖔𝖜𝖉𝖔𝖜𝖓

EARLY DECEMBER 1775

Refreshed from a couple of weeks away from Williamsburg's constant activity, Pendleton was delighted to be back among his colleagues. With only fifty-seven in attendance at the parish church of Richmond, he chose to stand before the convention delegates at pew-level rather than on the platform. The building's walls still echoed Henry's cry for liberty or death, while whispers that Robert C. Nicholas wanted to be relieved of his duty as president had made their rounds. Upon Peyton Randolph's death, his mantle had fallen to Nicholas but left the new leader troubled and jaded, leaving the convention to find a replacement. Pleased with Pendleton's management of the Committee of Safety, conservatives worked behind the scenes to assure he would be the one to step into the shoes of the president. A unanimous vote kept things moving along.

"Thank you, gentlemen," Pendleton said, "for the confidence you have placed in me. I will depend on your assistance to enable me to carry out my duties. Lord Dunmore's focus on Norfolk should allow

155

us to safely return to Williamsburg for the remainder of our meetings. I do not believe he would be willing to risk losing such a strategic hold in order to gain a lesser one. I am sure you are as anxious as I am to journey on to Williamsburg, so today's business will be brief."

Murmurs of affirmation went up from the group.

"There are rising concerns," Pendleton continued, "that the presence of Lord Dunmore and British soldiers in and around Norfolk will require additional American troops to keep them at bay. While Colonel Woodford is not inclined to accept the offer of assistance from those now stationed in North Carolina, I believe he should."

"I so move," one of the delegates said.

"Second," another chimed in.

"All in favor?" Pendleton said.

"Aye."

"Opposed?"

Silence.

"Then—"

One of the men rose from his seat. "I move that our convention's new president, Colonel Pendleton, be the one to write to Colonel Woodford asking him to embrace the offer."

Upon the delegate's approval of the motion, Pendleton placed the convention in adjournment, to reconvene at the college in Williamsburg at eleven o'clock the following Monday. "Those on the Committee of Safety shall remain here for a few hours to handle its affairs, but we will see the rest of you back in the capital next week."

With both the committee and convention to lead, there was no time to wonder if he had taken on too much. There were jobs to do, and he would do his best to honor the trust his beloved colony had placed in him.

Garbed in his colonel's uniform, Henry held his chin high. The brass buttons on his dark blue coat sparkled atop its forest green facing. With the convention back in Williamsburg only a week and Dunmore set to pounce, the time had come for Henry to make his move. He pressed his lips tight as he surveyed the half dozen men from the Committee of Safety who sat before him in the small meeting room. Today, facing Pendleton seemed less maddening than remaining idle. Action trumped waiting. Henry stiffened his legs and pushed back his shoulders as he stood unyielding before the group of men.

"North Carolina?" Heat crawled up Henry's neck, yet he refused to let his demeanor go unchecked. "Colonel Woodford will be reinforced with troops from North Carolina?"

Pendleton sat resolute on the other side of the table. Now, whether Henry turned to the convention or to the Committee of Safety, he must go through his nemesis. If only George Mason's health would improve and add a friendly face to those who sought to rule him with a rod of iron.

"Colonel Howe," Pendleton said, "offered his continentals to assist during our time of need. We cannot deny the success of the North Carolina troops and certainly have no reason to refuse their help."

Henry stared at the ceiling through squinted eyes before returning his gaze to the man who had been the leader of his opposition for more than a decade. "But no one knows when the remaining troops from North Carolina will arrive. My regiment is right here and ready to assist."

He clutched Woodford's letter. Had Henry's note to him been overly polite? No one could consider his request unreasonable. As commander in chief, he should expect the junior officer to supply him with intelligence he could convey to the convention. Yet Woodford replied he had kept the convention fully informed via multiple letters to Pendleton. The letter Henry held in his hand made the position of the subordinate officer clear. Woodford believed his responsibilities were to the Committee of Safety "as the supreme power" in Virginia and not to Henry, the "commanding officer of the troops at Williamsburg."

At Williamsburg? The convention had placed Henry over troops in the entire colony, not just those in Williamsburg.

Swallowing the bitter words that threatened to escape from his lips, Henry chose to address the committee with words seasoned with grace. "It is my understanding Colonel Woodford has requested that the greater part of the First Regiment march to the scene of the action. Immediately."

Pendleton sat in silence, hands resting by his side while his pale blue eyes remained unyielding. How could such a warmhearted soul refuse to listen to reason? The expressions of a couple men in the room reflected encouragement, so Henry pressed on.

"And based on the information you have received from Colonel Woodford"—Henry pushed the communication issues from the forefront of his mind—"Lord Dunmore appears ready to attack Norfolk at any time."

"We are following the situation and will adjust accordingly," Pendleton said.

Henry's mind reeled while he drew air in and out of his nostrils. If he had learned anything over the years, it was that with Pendleton the selection of words carried much weight, and a calm delivery reigned supreme. "Colonel Pendleton, I would like to propose that the committee consider utilizing at least some of my men for the protection of Norfolk."

Pendleton turned to the others on the committee. Several nodded. Pendleton pivoted back to Henry. "We will take this matter into consideration and call you back when we have reached a verdict."

Henry forced as genuine a smile as he could muster. "Thank you, sir." His heart thumped against his chest. Dare he continue? Would doing so put his request at risk? He knew not when he might have another opportunity to speak with the committee, so he gulped down a steadying breath, then continued. "If you will allow me to lay but one additional item before the committee."

Pendleton extended an open palm toward Henry.

"It has been of great concern to me," Henry said, "that, despite being selected as the commander in chief of the Virginia troops, I have not been kept informed of related activities which take place in this great colony of ours. Do you not believe that, as commander in chief, 'tis I to whom Colonel Woodford should be sending his reports?"

"We will also make that a topic of discussion." Pendleton rose from his chair, placing his fingertips on the tabletop before him. "Mr. Henry, I bid you a good day. We will discuss these matters and send word as soon as we have a response to your concerns."

Henry gave a clipped nod, turned on his heels, and departed. He had done what he could.

Now he must wait.

Pendleton pitched a glance toward Bland, who, at sixty-five, was the eldest of those gathered. Stern faces of other committee members confirmed this would be a battle all its own. Lasting scars and resentments were alive and well. While the earlier seven-to-four vote supported Pendleton, a shift could turn the tide in the wrong direction. Sending an inexperienced officer to the front lines could prove disastrous for the troops.

"Gentlemen," Pendleton said, "you have heard Mr. Henry's requests."

Joseph Jones, one of the more recent additions to the committee, squared his shoulders. "With all due respect, Colonel Pendleton, it is *Colonel* Henry, not *Mister* Henry."

Pendleton tilted his head in surrender and provided a thin smile. "My apologies. Colonel Henry."

"And it was he," Jones said, planting one fist on the table, "that the convention selected as Virginia's commander in chief. The committee had no authority to supply Colonel Woodford with a separate command and send him to Great Bridge in place of Colonel Henry."

Pendleton shuffled a few papers on the table before him, pulling one from the pile. "If we look at the ordinance, we see that"—Pendleton found the spot on the page which addressed the concern—"this committee 'shall have full power to direct and appoint stations, marches, and encampments. And all chief and commanding officers are hereby required to pay that strict obedience to such orders as they shall receive from the said Committee of Safety.'" He raised his head. "Even though this document was drawn up in haste, I'm sure that you, as a fellow attorney, appreciate the need for our committee to fulfill the commission given to us by the convention."

Bland stirred. "Besides, Colonel Henry's democratic approach leaves many less than certain that he has the abilities to carry out his command on a field of battle."

Jones leaned in. "If you would but take a look at his library—"

One of Pendleton's allies snapped a look at Jones. "Purchasing a book is not the same as reading it."

Jones's face reddened, and he began pushing himself to his feet.

Pendleton lifted a palm toward the men. "Gentlemen, although our differences of opinion are great, we must maintain a sense of calm. The lives of our troops depend on our making well-thought-out decisions, not those born out of haste or untamed zeal."

Another member nodded. "Colonel Henry's ability to rally the troops is well known, yet that does not necessarily translate to an ability to train them in the art of war. Seasoned officers believe his familiarity with the troops conflict with the need to maintain strict discipline among them."

"No one doubts Colonel Henry's courage," Pendleton said. "But as a committee, we must also demonstrate courage in the decisions we make. We did so with our decision to send the more qualified man, not the most popular one, to the front lines."

"For the purpose of elevating Colonel Woodford to a position of honor and prestige." Jones's voice came low and gruff.

Pendleton picked up one of the quills lying on the table before him, rose from his chair, and walked to the map hanging from the wall. "We must do what is best for the country and wise for the troops. I see no harm in sending perhaps three companies currently under Colonel Henry's command to join Colonel Woodford's regiment at Great Bridge." He brushed the feather end of the quill across the map from the capital to the scene of the current activities.

Jones leaned back in his chair. The wrinkles on his forehead began to fade.

"Those in favor?"

"Ayes" went up around the room.

Pendleton nodded. "Thank you for your willingness to come together for the sake of the cause. As for Colonel Henry's request regarding communication, I believe we should postpone that decision. With the urgency of the situation at Great Bridge and nearby Norfolk in danger, other matters must be pushed aside. As Virginia and North Carolina's lifeline to the rest of the world and Dunmore's only way to get necessary supplies, control of the bridge is crucial to both sides. We must keep our focus on securing it. With the term of this committee set to expire during this convention, the new committee can take up matters of communication after its election. I plan to provide the opportunity to vote within the next week or so.

"In the meantime, let us each pray for heaven to direct the bullets of our troops and to preserve our men from all designs of the wicked enemy. I will see to it that the necessary arrangements are made regarding both of these decisions. Good day, gentlemen."

Henry coiled his fingers into a ball, then tapped it against his leg to the beat of the drum. Mere hours separated his request from the committee's reply. And now, three of his companies, hauling five hundred pounds of powder and fifteen hundred pounds of lead, marched before him on their way out of Williamsburg. Leaving their leader behind. Their destination: Great Bridge, which spanned a branch of the Elizabeth River. His old friend Joseph Jones had joined him for the sendoff.

"Will the committee ever allow me to fully play out the role the convention bestowed on me?" Henry asked.

Jones kicked at the dirt. "Let me write to Colonel Woodford. Perhaps he will agree to a just and reasonable solution."

"I don't know."

"Give me a few days. If Woodford doesn't agree, I will suggest a compromise to the committee."

Henry questioned Jones with his look. "What kind of compromise?"

"At the last meeting, we reviewed your commission. I am afraid the haste with which it was written provided the Committee of Safety with more authority than we would have liked. The wording is strong, and with Colonel Pendleton's attention to detail, I don't believe we can get you what you want. Besides, General Washington speaks highly of Colonel Woodford."

"But what about the compromise?" Henry asked.

"Perhaps compromise is the wrong word," Jones said. "But if I ask them to allow you to give the orders and be Woodford's point of contact, except when the convention or committee is in session, it would preserve your honor."

Henry furrowed his brow. "But one or the other is always in session."

"Exactly. They can grant your requests, at least in theory, yet still get what they want. Complete control."

"Very well," Henry said. "But if both Woodford and the committee reject your requests, I plan to take my complaint to the convention itself. Even though Colonel Pendleton is in charge there, too, I would have a broader audience to hear my plea."

Jones nodded.

The final sixty-eight-man company moved past the two men, leaving five of Henry's eight companies behind. Perhaps Henry's men could make a difference at Great Bridge. With or without him.

CHAPTER 18

Norfolk Burns

MID-DECEMBER 1775 - EARLY JANUARY 1776

Hurrying down Duke of Gloucester Street toward the Randolph home, Pendleton pulled his coat tighter against mid-December's breeze. Aromas from the taverns' gingerbread cakes wafted by. Reflection on the *Gazette*'s open declaration of independence would have to wait, as would the search for Jack's missing horse. For now, ideas were forming as to how he would word the convention's declaration regarding the slaves to whom Lord Dunmore had offered freedom if they would fight on behalf of the Crown. He would encourage the people of Virginia to make known the convention's offer of mercy to those who had found themselves as a pawn in the royal governor's scheme. Thankfully, despite the General Assembly's earlier decision to make such actions punishable by death, the convention would pardon those who would immediately surrender to Colonel Woodford or to any other commander of troops under the direction of the committee.

"Colonel Pendleton?"

Pendleton looked over his shoulder, stopped his advance, and offered a word of greeting to the gentleman hastening toward him. The corners of Henry's coat flapped open in rhythm with the clop of each boot. He had done well to keep his tongue despite not playing a greater role in the victory at Great Bridge.

Henry halted a few feet from Pendleton and tipped his head in greeting. "If I could have but a moment of your time."

"Certainly," Pendleton said, "if you wouldn't mind walking with me." The two men fell into step. "What's on your mind?"

"I received additional word from Colonel Woodford regarding the battle at Great Bridge."

"Oh?" Pendleton sidestepped a pile of horse manure.

"He referred to the victory as a second Bunker's Hill, in miniature." Henry glanced down. "Of course, he mentioned the difference of our suffering only one man wounded, and that our men have been able to keep their post. And, apparently, your encouraging Colonel Woodford to treat the enemy with a sense of humanity has not gone unnoticed by the British troops, many of whom believed Lord Dunmore's prophecy to the contrary."

"Thank you," Pendleton said. "The convention unanimously approved his actions as well. It is unfortunate that more than a dozen British regulars and their leader are dead, not to mention the wounded. But it is the price the Motherland has decided to pay by continuing to reject our pleas for a peaceful settlement."

"You must be pleased with your family connections among the Culpeper militia," Henry said. "I'm sorry they had to endure such dreadful conditions in order to aid in the victory."

"They made me proud, and we are working to get our men more of the basic provisions." Pendleton rubbed his chin. "I'm afraid there is nothing we can do about the weather."

"Yes, sir. It was an amazing win for the first southern land battle of this conflict." Henry cleared his throat. "In order to hold onto our success, however, I believe the activity off the coast at Hampton deserves further inspection."

Pendleton stopped in his tracks. He nodded at Henry, whose patience had far outweighed what others could endure. Perhaps the time had come to loosen his grip a bit and give Henry an opportunity to prove himself. "I will be happy to speak with the committee about your going to investigate."

They resumed their walk and turned onto North Queen Street.

"Thank you, Colonel—"

An almost thunderous clippety-clop of hooves pulled the men's attention to behind them. One of their express riders pulled up beside Pendleton and Henry, his chest heaving as air filled his lungs.

Pendleton examined the face of the young man, but exhaustion masked any clues that might otherwise be present.

"It's Norfolk," the messenger sputtered between breaths. "The British troops, along with the local Tories, have evacuated and taken refuge aboard naval vessels just offshore. They have disarmed and abandoned the runaway slaves."

Pendleton's eyes widened. "And the city?"

"Colonel Howe and his troops from North Carolina, with the assistance of Colonel Woodford's men, have taken possession of Norfolk. About twelve hundred men in total."

A jolt of elation rushed through Pendleton's body, and Henry flashed a broad smile.

The messenger's countenance turned solemn. "Colonels Howe and Woodford want to know if they should expect provisions while holding onto Norfolk, or should it be totally destroyed?"

Pendleton's mind raced. Virginia's lifeline to the world, totally destroyed? "I will present the question to the convention as soon as possible. Thank you for the news. Come with me to provide additional details."

He pivoted toward Henry. "Meanwhile, you prepare to depart for Hampton. I will provide confirmation of your mission once I receive it."

"If I may be so bold . . ." Henry said.

Pendleton pinned his eyes on Henry.

"When do you believe the convention will make a decision regarding the formation of a navy?"

"There is much to discuss," Pendleton said. "But with the current state of affairs and a vote on the new Committee of Safety planned for tomorrow, I have little doubt we will take up the matter very soon. The next ten days will determine whether or not our Christmas will be a happy one."

The pungent smell of ink tickled Pendleton's nose as he returned the quill to its inkwell and leaned back in his chair. The fire from the hearth crackled. Christmas Eve landing on the Sabbath afforded Pendleton a few hours of peace on earth, albeit in Williamsburg and miles from loved ones back home. His fingers caressed the recent letter from his wife before turning his attention to the matters at hand.

The victory at Great Bridge and the retaking of Norfolk from Dunmore had been tempered by Pendleton nearly losing control of the Committee of Safety. If ever there was a time when the Henry-faction was alive at the convention, 'twas now. Despite their stirring up discontent regarding the committee's treatment of Virginia's commander in chief, the men had voted to keep Pendleton as their leader. Perhaps the convention's endorsement of Henry's push for a navy would provide some satisfaction for those who still believed Pendleton's decisions were primarily personal. They weren't. Lives and America's well-being were at stake, and Pendleton would do his best to protect both.

The addition of Henry's attorney friend to the committee had pushed it toward compromise. Still, a grin spread across Pendleton's face. The result would be the same. Woodford would not need to report to or be subjected to Henry so long as either the convention or the Committee of Safety was available. And one or the other would always be within reach.

Despite the friendship with Woodford blossoming over the years, this season presented its share of difficulties. Built upon a solid foundation, current circumstances—balancing Henry's official military role while striving to keep those on the front lines safe—posed challenges. Even so, Pendleton felt compelled to pick up his quill and make sure his friend not only received the resolution concerning Mr. Henry, but also reminders of the tenderness between them.

Ah, yes, Mr. Henry.

Although significant, Henry's success in securing precious salt from two merchant ships bound for Lord Dunmore during his time in Hampton was but a flash in the pan. Pendleton leaned into the desk and picked up the not-quite-finished letter to Colonel Woodford. Pendleton's eyes scanned until they came to the portion related to Henry.

The unlucky step of calling that gentleman from our councils where he was useful, into the field of an important station—the duties of which he must be an entire stranger to—has given me many anxious and uneasy moments. He has done nothing worthy of degradation and must keep his rank, yet his position of leadership deprives us of the services of some able officers, whose honor and former ranks will not suffer them to act under him.

A heartfelt groan escaped from Pendleton's lips. *But how we need their services now.*

Pendleton shifted his focus to a few lines down to what he had taken up his pen to convey: the matter of the committee's decision regarding what they would require of Woodford's relationship with Henry. Surely the compromise would be satisfactory to Woodford, but Pendleton could not resist making it clear that Virginia could not part with Woodford so long as troops were necessary.

Pendleton flexed his fingers. They ached, but he picked up his pen to ask that he be remembered to family and friends who served with Woodford. "I hope Jack Taylor is not among the refractory," he wrote, "but that everything in his power is done to make you happy."

A few more sentences, then he closed, "I have given you a long letter, the reading of which will prevent your wishing to receive another soon. You'll always believe, I hope, that I am Your very Affectionate Friend. Edmd Pendleton"

Pendleton sat back, taking a peek at the clock on the mantle. He must turn in for, Christmas or no Christmas, tomorrow would be work as usual in Virginia's capital city. Would Lord Dunmore's defeats at Great Bridge and Norfolk be enough to turn the governor away from his warlike measures?

Pendleton lifted himself out of the chair, giving a single nod to the men seated around the meeting room's oblong table. "Thank you again, gentlemen, for adjusting to the last-minute change in venue. We are grateful to the college for accommodating us. You will receive the time and place of our next meeting once those arrangements can be made. In the meantime, please pray this new year will provide a resolution."

The men pushed back from the table, then hurried off to tend to various aspects of their business. Pendleton collected his things and made his way to the hall spanning the west side of the building. He strolled to the top of the staircase, but movement from outside drew him to one of the icicle-laced windows. Henry's troops seemed to be forming a loose huddle at their campsite. What might the Son of Thunder be up to now?

Pendleton wrapped his coat snug about him, placed his hat on his head, then made his way down the stairs. A gust of frosty air greeted him as he stepped onto the portico. Shouldn't he be at home in Caroline enjoying a glass of the new year's punch with his family? He swept a glance down the large veranda. With some distance between him and the gathering, the shadow of one of the large arches gracing the building's outer edge would be enough to conceal his identity, yet provide a clear view. Situated, he pulled a handkerchief from his pocket and raised it to his nose to temper the smell of smoke still drifting in from Norfolk.

The unmistakable voice of Patrick Henry rose above the commotion. Pendleton shifted to a more comfortable position. If Virginia's military leader—Pendleton winced at the thought—was going to address his men, he needed to brace himself for another rousing speech. Pendleton squinted. Yes, Henry had pushed his spectacles to the top of his head.

Henry's raised hands calmed the scores of men standing before him. "I hope our countrymen will not be at all dispirited at the destruction of Norfolk but, rather, rejoice that half the mischief our enemies can do is done already. They have destroyed one of the first towns in America, and the primary one in Virginia which carries on anything like trade."

"Hear! Hear!" his admirers cheered.

Pendleton shifted his weight. Was it Lord Dunmore's irritation with the patriot troops taunting him from the shoreline, or had it been the provision-starved British troops that pushed him to order more than a hundred guns to open fire upon the town's waterfront buildings, inciting the American colonists to set the town ablaze? Three days of pillage and destruction had left more than two-thirds of Norfolk in ashes, making it difficult to argue that any of the town's assets remained. Yet the committee was divided as to how to proceed.

Norfolk. A rage swept over Pendleton. Only Lord Dunmore could do such a horrid work as to burn that great city to the ground.

Pendleton jerked his head and refocused his attention on Henry.

"We are only sharing part of the sufferings of our American brethren," Henry proclaimed, "and can now glory in having received one of the keenest strokes of the enemy, without flinching." Henry strode across his imaginary, albeit grassy, stage, with chin held high. "They have done their worst. And to what purpose? To harden our soldiers and teach them to bear, without dismay, all the most formidable operations of a war carried on by a powerful and cruel enemy."

"We will fight!" someone from the crowd shouted.

"Huzzah!" those around him responded.

Pendleton leaned his shoulder into the arch's supporting structure, cold and rocklike, and narrowed his eyes. Britain's atrocities held no excuse, but had the Motherland gone so far as to be considered their cruel enemy? He didn't want to believe it, yet something within him churned.

Henry hunched over. "To no other purpose than to give the world examples of British cruelty. And of American fortitude." He lifted his frame and whirled to face the dozens of men behind him as he raised his index finger. "Unless it be to force us to lay aside that childish fondness for Britain, and that foolish, tame dependence on her."

"Aye!" someone growled.

Should Pendleton consider it childish the fondness he held for Britain, the one who had birthed the colonies into existence? He chewed on his lip. The smoke drifting in from Norfolk did little to convince him that nothing had changed or that any hope of redress remained.

Henry nodded and offered up a grin to his men. "We have borne so long restrictions to our trade. Our patience for their taxes and other acts of tyranny served but to encourage them to proceed to greater lengths—as far as their lust of despotism, stimulated by cruelty, could hurry them. How sunk is Britain!"

Pendleton shook his head. Britain had indeed turned against her colonies, but had Henry not considered the consequences of rushing into the fray against the mightiest navy in the world? Not doing so would only serve to make matters worse, not better, for those they had sworn to protect.

Henry continued to captivate his listeners. "Could not Britons venture to wage war with America till they were told that Americans were cowards, till they had disarmed them, or had, as they thought, put it out of their power to procure arms? Their reach extended so far as to attempt to raise domestic enemies among us by way of our Roman Catholic and Indian neighbors. If they were determined to conquer America, why did they not attempt it like Britons? Why meanly run to the different powers of Europe, entreating them not to assist us? Why make use of every base and inhuman scheme and wage a savage war unknown amongst civilized nations?

"Whoever has heard of the plots against us by Dunmore and others cannot but assume they have been authorized by a higher power. And whoever believes this cannot but wish to be forever removed from under such a power and to be guarded most effectually against it. Most freely would I cut the Gordian knot"—Henry swung an imaginary sword through the air—"which has hitherto bound us to Britain and call on France and Spain for assistance against an enemy who seems bent on our destruction."

Pendleton's heart pounded in his throat. Dare he admit, after decades of devotion and service to her, that the Motherland was bent on the colonies' destruction? The thought that the Motherland would abandon any hope of a peaceful resolution shook him to the core, yet her words and conduct left little room for doubt. Pendleton's fingernails dug into his palms.

The one to whom he had been faithful had broken their trust.

Ever the showman, Henry paused and circled around, catching the eyes of all he could before he continued. "But who, blessed be God of Hosts, has been baffled in most of their attempts against us, been chastised in all, and has made many attacks upon us without being able to kill a single man." Henry bowed to his cheering audience.

Pendleton let the wintry air fill his lungs before mumbling. "Without being able to kill a single man, indeed." He cast a parting glance at Henry and his troops before turning back to the college. "If Mr. Henry has his way, Britain will lay thousands of colonists at his feet—dead."

CHAPTER 19

Common Sense?

February 1776

Several days ride from North Carolina had chilled Penn to the bone, and February's weather had made ruts in the roads even worse. Nonetheless, thoughts he held from the late Christmas celebration with family warmed his heart. More days of travel lie ahead before he would arrive back in Philadelphia, but for now, he would soak in those memories and the comforts of his cousin's home. Penn rubbed his hands, then held them against the glow of the parlor's fireplace. Flickers of light danced across the room's floors and walls while the longcase clock just beyond the doorway advised the two men of the late hour. "I am grateful my adopted colony was able to be of service."

Pendleton leaned forward in his wingback chair. "And we thank you."

An unfamiliar awkwardness hung in the air, not matching the words flowing from his cousin's lips. Penn drew in his arms and pivoted to face his kinsman. "Are you well?"

Pendleton blinked. "Well?"

"Yes, are you well?" Penn said. "You have not been yourself since I arrived."

"Yes, as well as this aging body will allow." Pendleton's eyes locked with Penn's. "I am sorry, son. I suppose my mind is filled with all that needs to be done."

"These are turbulent times. Perhaps I should not have put you out in this way."

"Heavens, no." Pendleton rose from his chair, ambled over to the window, and pulled back a corner of the curtain. Moonbeams shimmered across the thin blanket of snow. "You are not the trouble. The trouble is out there. But, unfortunately, it has found its way into each of our souls." Pendleton turned back to Penn. "The attack on Norfolk and our defeat at Quebec cannot be taken lightly."

Penn nodded. "With North Carolina's governor calling on those loyal to the king to take up arms against their Whig brethren, it may only be a matter of time before the fighting reaches my colony." Penn paused, then caught himself before revealing too much. He would remain quiet about murmurs of independence which had tickled his ears in recent days. He longed to share his private battles with his cousin and wrestle through them together. But that door had not opened during this visit, and his instincts held him back.

"You may be right. Rest assured, we will not keep Colonel Howe and his troops here any longer than either of us believes is necessary."

"I know you won't," Penn said.

Pendleton returned his gaze to the window.

"I should retire for the night and let you be about your work." Penn held his hands to the fire one last time.

"But—"

"No, I must." Penn walked over to his host and placed a hand upon his arm. "It has been a long day, and my fragile frame will appreciate the rest. I will leave for Philadelphia before sunup."

Though the few days nestled in the pleasures of his Caroline County home had been good, a weariness accompanied Pendleton on his return to Williamsburg. A stillness had settled over the Randolph home for the evening, leaving Pendleton alone with his thoughts in the familiar guest chambers.

He bent low over the mahogany secretary desk, quill in hand. Although wishing to dwell on snippets of conversation with Penn from earlier in the month, concerns over King George, Lord Dunmore, and Patrick Henry pushed them aside. Pendleton lay down his quill and flexed his fingers. He scanned the few sentences already penned as the committee's reply regarding Dunmore's desire to negotiate. How Pendleton wished he could settle the matter with a few strokes of the pen, but that authority lay with the representatives meeting in Philadelphia. Congress would need to await a reply from the king regarding the recent petition they had sent to him.

Pendleton dipped his quill into the inkwell then touched it to the page. "If the administration is disposed to heal this unnatural wound in the empire, they will embrace that occasion"—Pendleton drew in a thoughtful breath before he continued—"which, probably will be the last of accomplishing it." He leaned back in his chair. Surely his Majesty would realize the darkness of the hour and provide an olive branch for the colonists to grab onto.

Some in Virginia already had whispers of war upon their lips. And sentiments from a pamphlet circulating in Philadelphia seemed to have turned whispers into all out cries for war. But was its author's reasoning really common sense as the title implied? His arguments had rattled around in Pendleton's head since he read them.

"The period of debate is closed," the pamphlet declared. But was it? Were the hopes for reconciliation they had embraced prior to fires being shot at Lexington now as useless as last year's almanac? Had a monarchy become tyrannical and unnecessary? Pendleton's stomach coiled into a knot. Could whoever authored the pamphlet have been right?

The argument that burned deepest within Pendleton's soul: Anything short of separation and independence would leave the sword to America's children. Although God had taken the only child given to him by blood, blessings now flowed from the Lord through the young men whose lives he had been privileged to touch. Would their offspring be forced to bear the sword if their fathers refuse to do so now? Already Jack Taylor and Henry Pendleton stood in harm's way.

Word had arrived that some in Congress were pushing for a formal declaration of independence and balked at those who continued to believe the administration would eventually produce honorable proposals. Pendleton's heart told him to believe the colonies already stood as independent in so many practical ways, yet his head knew otherwise.

From the corner of the desk, a two-week-old newspaper caught his eye. Had Lord Dunmore slipped when he made Lord North's conditions for peace public? Would Pendleton be included with the leaders the colonists would be required to deliver up, even though his efforts for reconciliation had been endless? The king's accusation that the colonies aimed at independence had not made Pendleton's push for a peaceful remedy any easier. And delegates in Philadelphia were receiving pressure from back home to submit to the chatter surrounding the pamphlet's so-called logic now permeating the colonies.

Had the destruction of Virginia's own port city not demonstrated the serious consequences of war? A weight settled on Pendleton's heart. His own role in calling for Norfolk's final annihilation was almost more than he could bear. Yet, after much debate, his committee had decided in mid-January that the remaining destruction of the town would be best. Any remaining buildings might provide comfortable lodging for the enemy. Reports had come that provided a glimmer of hope. One lone building remained standing. A church.

Rumbles within his own committee indicated some were now mentally ready for war, but slowness regarding physical preparations gave them pause. Despite the scarcity of both powder and lead, they chose to send part of Virginia's stock of powder to those in need in North Carolina. In addition, they supported Colonel Howe's decision to lead his fighting men back to Virginia's neighboring colony where the need had made the troop's return vital.

Pendleton clenched his aching fingers into his palm, then released one finger at a time. They throbbed from laboring over correspondence the day before, including one to Colonel Howe's replacement for the troops that remained. Patrick Henry, quiet for several weeks, had not been a consideration. And, if Colonel Woodford would remain firm, the committee could continue to lean on him, rather than on Mr. Henry.

The candle on the corner of the desk nearly burned down to a nub, Pendleton rose from the chair. His concerns followed him as he made final preparations for the night.

What would happen once an answer arrived from Philadelphia regarding the convention's request that Congress take all of Virginia's troops into continental service? Would they want Henry to continue in a leadership role or would Virginia's questions regarding his abilities have somehow reached their ears? Pendleton pushed the thought from his mind, blew out the candle, and crawled into bed.

He drifted off to sleep, lifting up a final prayer for the Lord to intervene.

Henry stood before the Committee of Safety, his shoulders pushed back and the decision made. Today he would make his intensions known. More than five months had come and gone since the mid-September day when Virginia had sworn in Henry as its commander in chief. And now, he had been summoned so that he might formally receive his military commission issued by Congress, which would place him under the command of former subordinates. It would be his to accept or reject. The words Washington spoke to him months before came rushing back. *Remember, Mr. Henry, what I now tell you: From the day I enter upon the command of the American armies, I date my fall, and the ruin of my reputation.* Was this now happening to him?

The morning light produced an odd glow upon the document Pendleton held out for Henry. He glanced around at the nearly dozen men, then allowed his eyes to move toward the paper that would determine his destiny. The moments dragged by as he reviewed the words before him. He collected his thoughts, then raised his head to address the committee.

"Gentlemen, I am unable to accept this commission."

Pendleton provided a slight nod. "So be it. I will instruct the commissary to issue to you the balance due."

Henry tipped his head in acknowledgement, then turned to leave.

Never would Henry have imagined spending the day at Raleigh Tavern for a farewell dinner—at the insistence of his troops. Former troops.

Aromas from the curried catfish lingered while the tavern's guests enjoyed their chocolate pudding. Light from the hearth's flames reflected against somber eyes of the men seated around the tables scattered about the room.

Flames dancing in the fireplace drew Henry's gaze to the Latin engraving above the mantle. How often had he appreciated the reminder, "Jollity is the offspring of wisdom and good living"? Yet today the reference to jollity mocked the black bands wrapped around the left arms of his men. A weak smile touched Henry's lips. The armbands revealed the men's heartfelt mourning. While Henry remained alive and well, the stench of death hovered about him—the death of his short-lived military career.

Henry pushed his attention back to the closing remarks of the man standing before them.

"So, Colonel Henry," the soldier said, spreading his arms wide toward those seated around the room, "we say once again that being under your command has truly been an honor and that your withdrawing from service has filled us with the most poignant sorrow."

Shouts of support went up around the room.

"Hear, hear!" someone said with a raised fist.

"No finer man could lead us!" another chimed in.

Henry pushed back from the table and hoisted himself to his feet. He soaked in the moment, then held up a hand to quiet the group. "Gentlemen, your address does me the highest honor. And you are to be commended for the spirit and zeal you have constantly shown in your various stations." He pivoted to face those behind him. "Rest assured, although I depart the service, I leave my heart with you. May God bless you, give you success and safety, and make you the glorious instruments of saving our country."

Around the room, chair legs scraped against the wooden floor as men jumped to their feet. Servants carrying dinnerware shuffled to avoid collision.

"We'll give him the proper and most glorious escort out of town!"

"The best this town has ever seen!"

Warmth rushed to Henry's cheeks.

"We will fetch you an appropriate chariot for the occasion," someone offered.

Several men howled. Others banged their fists on the tables.

"But first we will all demand our own discharge!"

"Aye! We will serve under none but thee, Colonel Henry!"

The men poured from the tavern into the streets, their commotion rambling up the road toward the barracks.

A host of emotions tumbled through Henry like a choppy river over its rocks. His throat went dry, then he levied a look of confusion at his lieutenant. "Did they just threaten to refuse to serve?"

His lieutenant nodded.

The men who remained pulled him toward exit and the honorable escort they had promised.

Henry's thoughts tumbled one over the other as he pushed the men away. "No, I cannot. Not until I have set my men straight." He raced across the room toward the door as his men fell in behind him. He reached the exit, whipped around, and threw up his arms, causing some to almost topple onto the floor.

"Men, yesterday's actions were motivated by my honor alone, and although I am prevented from serving my country in a military capacity, I will exert my utmost abilities in the interests of these United Colonies. And I must implore you all to continue to support the glorious cause in which you are currently engaged. I insist upon it."

Henry traded a glance with his lieutenant who had followed on his heels. "Come with me. We must find the others and bring them back into the fold."

CHAPTER 20

Matters are Drawing to a Crisis

FEBRUARY - MARCH 1776

Penn shook his head as he sauntered to the front of the empty wagon. The Southerner pulled his coat tight around his throat to guard against February's gusty winds and Philadelphia's icy streets. So far from home.

Penn patted the horse's rump, then looked up at the driver. "The powder isn't proper for what we need, so I am afraid your mission will be delayed. Stay nearby, and I will be in touch as soon as things have been sorted out. We must get these supplies to North Carolina soon."

The driver nodded, released the brake, then clicked his team of horses into motion.

"Mr. Penn?"

Penn spun around to see the Adams cousins weaving toward him through the townsfolk who had ventured out during the midday sun.

Samuel's smile eased wide. "We heard you were back in town."

"Just arrived." Penn cast a questioning look at John. "But I did not know you had returned."

John nodded. "Just returned myself. My cousin and I were heading to City Tavern to warm ourselves with some victuals. Samuel will catch me up on what has been happening while I was away. Care to join us?"

"I could use the nourishment," Penn said.

"Care to tell us what's going on?" Samuel tilted his head toward the wagon as it rolled away.

Penn extended his arm in the direction of the tavern, and the trio fell into step as they crossed the cobblestone street. "Some say a fire will soon be kindled in North Carolina, and they are in desperate need of supplies."

"A wagon without freight does not look encouraging."

"No, indeed." Penn cast a sideways glance at his companions. "I was under the impression powder, drums, and other supplies were ready to send, but the magazine only housed cannon powder which was coarse and ordinary. And the arms and saltpeter have not yet arrived."

"So, the battle is moving south?" John asked.

The men halted for a passing carriage, then resumed their stroll toward the source of the delectable smells wafting by them.

"My North Carolina colleague, Mr. Hooper, is in New York and has reason to believe General Clinton is heading to our colony. The good news seems to be that Mr. Hooper has awakened to the cause— or is at least finally aware we must take up arms in order to have a chance of preserving our freedom." They turned the corner, and the tavern came into view. "But enough of that for now. We need to hear Mr. Adams's updates in order to be ready for tomorrow's assembly."

Once inside, the three men settled into the chairs around one of the only available tables, then placed their orders. Attendants weaved around tables of all shapes and sizes, already filled with delegates humming with conversation.

Penn fixed his gaze on Samuel. "So?"

"Well," Samuel began, "after the two of you left, things were pretty quiet around here until a month ago."

John shifted his focus to Penn. "My cousin tells me the new pamphlet caused quite the stir in this town. I was able to obtain a copy during my journey here."

Samuel nodded. "Before its appearance, Congress did what it could to suppress the idea of independence. Then, last month, word came of the king's opening speech to Parliament in October. The same day, we learned of the destruction of Norfolk. On the heels of that news, the pamphlet made its way from the printing press to us."

"Do we know who wrote it?" Penn asked.

"Some think it was Dr. Franklin," Samuel said, "but he has denied it. For two weeks, Congress refused to acknowledge its existence. But a couple weeks ago, they formed a committee to explore the idea of independence."

John leaned in. "I like the title. *Common Sense*."

Penn pulled his arms away from the table to make room for the feast being spread before them. "But what did it say?" A prick behind his eyes caught him off guard. This would not be a good time for a headache.

"'Tis several pages long." Samuel pushed his rainbow trout aside. "But it focuses on two things. The Crown and the British constitution."

"But the king has not been the problem," Penn said. "Parliament has."

Samuel reached into his pocket. "I carry extra copies with me and would be more than happy to give you one."

Penn hesitated, then reached for the pamphlet.

The lodging room of the tavern, although more than adequate, kept Penn many miles away from those he loved on this Valentine's Day. How he wished to spend time writing to family of his thoughts of them rather than to others of hostilities that had come to the colonies' doorstep. He picked up the pamphlet and perused a couple of the arguments that had occupied his mind since Mr. Adams had given it to him.

The blood of the slain, the weeping voice of nature cries out, 'Tis time to part.... Reconciliation is now a fallacious dream.

Penn placed the pamphlet on a nearby chair, then pushed himself away from the desk and to his feet. He ambled over to the window and pulled the curtains tighter, then closed his eyes. The pamphlet would make its way to his cousin in Virginia. Would it stir him as it had so many in Philadelphia? Stir him enough to change course?

Penn's first week back in Philadelphia had flown by. On his first day back in Congress, divine appointment must have placed him and John Adams on the same committee to allow for additional conversations. Penn's eyes fluttered opened. He rubbed his fingers against his temples, then returned to his chair at the desk. Despite his throbbing head, he must finish the letter to Thomas Person, a good friend with whom he had bonded at North Carolina's Provincial Congress.

Pushing other papers out of the way, Penn retrieved the duplicate of the letter he wrote to Person two days prior. His eyes fell on key aspects of what he had conveyed.

General Clinton left Boston about three weeks ago .... I make no doubt but the Southern provinces will soon be the scene of action, as our enemies may hope to obtain greater success there as that at the northward .... The people to the northward have spirit and resolution which I doubt not will carry them victorious through this contest. I hope we to the southward shall act like men determined to be free.

Will it not be necessary for the convention to meet sooner than May in order to consult what steps may be needed for you to take?

He scanned down to the logistical matters.

I expect the wagon with powder, drums, etc., will be set off this week. Are there any preparations for making saltpeter, gunpowder or guns? The House of Commons have approved of the king's speech and promised to support him. Should they persevere in their attempts to reduce us to slavery, we must determine to act with unanimity.

He picked up the letter, then focused on its closing remarks.

Please remember me to my friends to whom I had not time to write. For God sake my good sir, encourage our people, animate them to dare even to die for their country.

Penn turned his gaze to today's letter he had already begun. In it, he assured his friend that Virginians would be ready and willing to assist them in whatever matter occasioned it. Now he would reveal his heart. The results of months of internal struggles must be openly expressed on paper.

He drew the quill from its well and began to write, eyes at half-mast from the pain behind them. "Matters are drawing to a crisis. These are serious things and require your consideration. The consequence of making alliances is perhaps a total separation with Britain."

Penn lifted his chin from the page for a moment to let his words sink in. The previous day's report in Congress had brought clarity. "My first wish," he wrote, "is that America may be free. The second, that we may be restored to peace and harmony with Britain upon just and proper terms."

There. On paper. Settled. Relief swept over him like a flood.

He picked up the pamphlet and laid it on the desk before adding a postscript. "I send you a pamphlet called *Common Sense* published here about a month ago." Penn returned the quill to its well, then sat back. His index finger tapped the words in the document he had read over and over again: "The period of debate is closed. Arms, as the last resource, must decide the contest."

"Perhaps this will bring clarity to them," Penn whispered, "as it has to me."

Philadelphia's streets came to life as winter's grip began to loosen. Though it took a month of wrangling, late March produced another wagon ready to send south. Penn patted the supplies it held while his North Carolina colleagues walked around to his side.

"These may or may not reach North Carolina before the new general arrives," Penn said, "but at least he will know they are on the way."

William Hooper nodded as he surveyed the load. "The Carolinas and Georgia will be glad to receive the powder, and with the drums and colors you sent a couple weeks ago—"

Joseph Hewes wagged his head. "I'm sure I mentioned that one of the best horses on the earlier wagon cut one of his hind feet during the journey. He must be replaced lest the supplies never reach their intended destination." He slumped onto a nearby boulder, gave his arms a brisk rub, and blew into the frosty air that surrounded him. "Never was any person more unfortunate than I have been in executing this order. And it is still not complete."

Penn meandered over and placed a hand on Hewes's shoulder. "You have done a fine job, Mr. Hewes. No one can accuse you of doing less than what is within your power to do. I'm sure General Lee will be glad to receive whatever he can get."

Hewes offered up a less-than-enthusiastic smile. "Nothing could be as dreadful as the Motherland removing the colonies from under the protection of the Crown."

The weight of Hewes's words hung midair for several moments before Penn replied. "The news is quite disturbing."

Hooper stared into the distance. "I'm afraid the news we received from North Carolina is no better."

"True," Penn said. "Nothing can compare with the blood that was shed at Moore's Creek Bridge, even though we were the victors."

"We?" Hooper said.

Penn shuffled his feet. "It is a bit baffling, wouldn't you say—our fellow colonists fighting amongst themselves? But what can you expect with our governor calling upon the Loyalists, not to mention the Scottish Highlanders, to take up arms against their Whig brethren?"

Hewes stood, with arms still crossed in front of him. "It seems nothing is left but to fight it out."

The words stung. Penn kicked the ground. "Spring's thaw is not far away. Mr. Hewes, I'm sorry you have decided not to journey with me home in time for our colony's Provincial Congress. It is time we find out for ourselves what has transpired in the hearts and minds of the people, especially the Tories, since we left."

Hewes shuddered. "Nothing would please my constitution more than an excuse not to sit in a stationary chair for hours on end, day in and day out. But the drivers tell me the roads are bad and the journey difficult." Hewes glanced at Hooper. "At the moment, Mr. Hooper is more fit than I for such a trip."

Penn's focus drifted to Hooper. "Mr. Hooper?"

"I have traveled a number of miles in recent weeks," Hooper said, "and would love nothing more than to sit still, even as Mr. Hewes described. But it seems present circumstances dictate the trip may be for the two of us, Mr. Penn."

"Then it's settled," Penn said. "We will make the necessary preparations and leave as soon as reasonably possible." From the corner of his eye, he caught sight of a familiar figure moved toward them, waving a piece of paper. "John Adams?"

"Good day, gentlemen," Adams said. "I see your efforts to obtain supplies has finally reaped a satisfactory outcome."

Hewes grunted.

"Yes, indeed," Penn said. "But you have raised my curiosity. Does the paper you carry have anything to do with our prior discussions?"

"It is not yet complete," Adams said. "But I am working on it as I am able."

Hewes tilted his head. "And what, may I ask, is it?"

Adams lips pulled into a smile as he held up the paper. "Mr. Hooper and Mr. Penn requested that I put together my thoughts regarding the formation of a new government. Their friends back home would like something to review at North Carolina's upcoming Congress." Adams glanced down at the paper. "This is a proposal I have been working on but have kept relatively quiet until now. It is not yet ready for the general public, or even for Congress, but with your special request . . ."

Penn looked at Hewes. "Since the author of *Common Sense* encouraged us to think about setting up our own government, Mr. Adams has taken action on the matter." Penn turned toward Adams. "Mr. Adams, when do you think it will be ready?"

Adams's eyes tightened at the corner. "With so much time spent in meetings these days, it is hard to say. But perhaps soon."

"It won't be long before Mr. Hooper and I will be heading south," Penn said.

"Then," Adams said, "I shall burn the midnight oil, if needed. If I am unable to get it to you before you leave, I shall send it along as soon as it is ready."

Penn nodded, a spark of excitement rushing through him. "Very well then, we will look forward to receiving it."

CHAPTER 21

Battered Roads

April 1776

Pendleton sat in the front hall of the governor's palace along with his friend and fellow committee member Mr. Bland. What a relief that the doubts of Bland's loyalty to America had proven false, and their friendship remained intact. Night had fallen, yet additional matters needed attention before the day could come to a close. Pendleton's light jacket provided little warmth inside the makeshift military command post, whose chill extended beyond its lack of heat. Embers from the fireplace cast an eerie glow against the walls of the roundish room, which served as a reception area for guests. Where long muskets and swords once adorned the spaces above the mantel and large doors, discolored shadows remained. Amid the current state of affairs, all weapons had been removed to be evaluated for potential use. The black and white marble floor stood in stark contrast to the shell of a room once meant to impress.

The place reeked. Pendleton reached into his pocket for a handkerchief, then patted his nose, but the musty odor prevailed. Had the servants not aired out the general's attire from his waterlogged arrival a few days before?

Pendleton rubbed his arms for warmth. What was keeping the general? The brief time he had spent with the committee had been enough to magnify the differences between them.

Much had transpired since Henry's courteous, albeit festive, departure from his military rank a month before. But what Henry laid down on his way out of town, the newspaper had picked up. For weeks, Pendleton bore the weight of accusations regarding how he managed Henry in his role as commander in chief. Despite attempts to set the record straight, in private and with a gentle touch, there were those who refused to listen to reason.

The aging Bland slumped in his chair. "Do you suppose the general has forgotten my referring to the author of *Common Sense* as a blockhead and ignoramus?"

Pendleton traded a sympathizing glance with his friend. "We are in this together."

"You were right, you know," Bland said. "America is safer with Henry's newfound civilian status. I heard that both General Washington and Colonel Jefferson expressed relief."

Pendleton provided a lone nod.

"As for Mr. Henry's belief that you and the committee were responsible for Congress offering him a demotion, we know otherwise. None of us ever sought to interfere with their choice of officers."

"We even warned them, didn't we?" Pendleton stared into the blackness of one of the floor tiles. "But at times, misunderstanding, or even a scarred reputation, is the price of leadership. It is the people, not ourselves, that we serve."

"Gentlemen." The address from the general's military aide pulled the men from their reflections. "The general will see you now."

Pendleton and Bland rose as General Charles Lee entered the hall.

The general's slender body and towering stature conveyed a sense of imbalance, yet somehow fit his role as military commander of the Southern Colonies.

The general jabbed a finger at the two chairs from which the gentlemen had risen. The two lowered back into them as the general launched in. "I assume this will be brief. There are numerous things to which I must attend."

Pendleton mustered up a smile. "No doubt, General." He shifted in his chair, swallowing the words that threatened to escape. The less the general knew about the misconceptions of his constituents back home regarding how he had handled Henry's brief military career, the better. "Your presence here in the capital will allow me the opportunity to tend to those matters which require my attention back in Caroline. With your blessing, and once the committee feels comfortable with my leaving, I will depart."

The general took a few steps away from Pendleton and Bland, and cleared his throat. "It is no secret that I do not mince words." He spun around to face his guests, his owl-like nose difficult to ignore. "My time here has convinced me that the Provincial Congress of New York consists of angels of decision when compared with the so-called Committee of Safety in Williamsburg."

Heat crept up Pendleton's neck. Barking, from the general's pack of dogs outside the walls of the palace, filled the silence.

Pendleton took a breath through his nostrils, forcing a strained smile. "I assure you, General, the committee has been very thoughtful and deliberate in every decision it has made over the past many months. And we have always kept in mind the people we represent."

General Lee shot a narrow-eyed look at the two men. "I'm sure. Yet timidity has no place in military maneuvers."

Pendleton's jaw tightened. Prudence would have been a better word choice than timidity, but saying so would merely add kindling to the general's well-known fiery temper. Pendleton kept his tongue. The nickname given to the general by the tribe of his Mohawk wife had been a proper one—Boiling Water.

"Until quite recently," Pendleton said, looking up at the general, "redress, rather than independence, has been the focus of those meeting in Philadelphia."

A sneer pulled at the general's cheek. "Regardless, you may take your leave. I have everything under control here."

Bland jumped in. "General Lee, I am sure you will keep Colonel Pendleton aware of any military-related activities while he is away."

The general's face never softened. "I will. If that is all, I must be about my business."

Pendleton rose and tipped his head toward the general, who was already marching from the room. Pendleton extended a hand of assistance to his friend. "Shall we go? I believe we can find fresher air elsewhere."

Penn pulled at his horse's reins, his body complaining from the many miles traveled. Hewes had been right. The winter-battered roads had proven more than challenging. While conversations with Hooper concerning John Adams's letter had been stimulating, Penn longed for his own bed and all the conveniences his home would afford.

As the familiar one-and-a-half-story tavern came into view, Penn tugged at his horse's reins. "It's here for the night."

Hooper dipped his chin in agreement. "The road has not been kind to us."

"Perhaps Mr. Adams was right that the greatest philosophers and lawgivers of antiquity would have wished to live in our time. But my constitution believes they would have preferred to form their new government while sitting still rather than traveling these many miles."

Hooper pulled his horse to a stop and dismounted.

Penn remained in his saddle, soaking in the stillness that came over his body. Indeed, in all of history, very few had the opportunity of choosing a system of government for themselves and their children. But must the journey be so long and arduous in getting there? Adams had declared that virtue, rather than fear, should be the center of government. *A wise man.*

Servants emerged from the stable to tend to the horses, and Penn dismounted. The ground hardly felt stable beneath his feet, so he placed one hand on his beast.

"Are you alright?" Hooper asked.

"I just need a minute."

"It seems your spirit," Hooper said, "rather than your body, is carrying you through."

"The spirit of John Locke and others who have come before us."

The tavern door swung open, and out stepped Thomas Person, the innkeeper.

"You are a sight for sore eyes," Penn said.

"A good journey?" Person asked.

Hooper glanced at Penn. "Let's just say we are happy to be this close to home."

"'Tis a much different place than the one you left two months ago," Person said.

Penn nodded. "We have heard nothing but talk of independence throughout Virginia." He grabbed some dry clothes out of his saddle, then the three men headed toward the shelter of the inn.

"If my traveling guests can be taken at their word," Person said, "I think you will find the same in North Carolina. All fondness for the king or for Britain has disappeared. The governors using the slaves as pawns, coupled with the late act of Parliament, has not been to their favor."

Penn's eyes widened. "Times are changing, and if they are as you say, my colleague and I will be ready to communicate these findings as soon as we return to Philadelphia." Already, a letter to John Adams was forming in his mind.

Other delegates, especially those from Virginia, must be told of the transformation taking place in their own colony. Something within Penn ached. What of his cousin Edmund Pendleton? Would he be ready to change with the times, or would he continuc to cling to his deep-rooted loyalties to the Motherland?

Papers scattered about Pendleton's desk in the Randolph's guest room confirmed that he was back in Williamsburg. Memories of the couple weeks he enjoyed at home were washed away in a town wrought with issues. Issues of General Lee's making. Protests from members of the Committee of Safety had made their way to Pendleton regarding Lee's redistribution of troops. Pendleton responded by writing a polite letter to the general reminding him of the role of the committee, once again under Pendleton's command. Lee's converting the college into a military hospital without the committee's involvement gave the impression that the people were under a military government.

"Heavens," Pendleton said in a hushed tone, "was he unable to see the conflict?" In the days since Pendleton had returned to Williamsburg, he noticed a difference in the general's conduct. Using more carefully chosen words, Lee's demeanor hinted at kindness and remorse for how he had treated Pendleton and for how he had responded to the actions of the committee.

Pendleton fingered the edge of one piece of parchment which represented the more pressing matter that lie before him. Resolutions from various colonies. More and more, Britain's semblance of mercy and feeble attempts at reconciliation had become a thin veil under which the pursuit of enslaving her colonies attempted to hide. Penn's adopted home, North Carolina, had released its delegates to go along with the other colonies if they chose to declare independence. Massachusetts, South Carolina, and even Georgia had taken a similar course. Would other colonies follow suit?

Virginia's Fifth Convention would begin in a matter of days. Would they once again select Pendleton to lead them? Pendleton lifted his eyes in silent prayer. The American colonies had chosen the path he had fought against for so long. If elected, would he have the wisdom and grace to lead the way?

CHAPTER 22

The Edge of Ruin
May 6 - 14, 1776

Henry skirted the hearth, pacing back and forth in the parlor of the governor's palace. Although the first session of Virginia's Fifth Convention would begin in less than an hour, he would not let General Lee's arguments deter him from expressing his growing concerns. "But if Britain hears of our making a formal declaration before Congress too soon, they will surely anticipate Americans seeking cooperation at the French court. We must declare our independence, yet the order of our actions is paramount."

The general leaned forward in his chair. "My arguments are in no way designed to benefit me. I assure you, if independence is declared, no man on this continent will suffer any more from the separation than I."

Henry halted, stole a peek at the longcase clock whose oblong frame mimicked the nearby windows, then resumed pacing. "Until we have felt the pulse of both France and Spain, perhaps we should postpone our declaration."

The general stood, took two steps forward, and planted himself in front of Henry. He placed a hand on Henry's shoulder and looked him square in the eye. "Mr. Henry, I am not at liberty to say how they know this, but before I departed Philadelphia, the Committee of Secrecy conveyed to me that the pulse of each has been taken and found to be in our favor." The general removed his hand and turned his gaze to the ceiling. "Admittedly, we run the risk of a cold reception to such a declaration but, I believe, the time for taking that risk is now."

Silence hung in the air before Henry replied. "We are talking about facing Britain's navy, the most powerful marine force in the world."

A sly grin spread across the general's face. "A force whose power has been established upon England's trade with America. A trade which they have shut down to bring America to her knees. I believe their action may have the reverse effect."

Words Henry had spoken before the convention in Richmond a year before now haunted him. Words that pushed back against Pendleton's warning not rush to war before securing foreign alliances. Alliances that could help protect the colonies against the impending storm. Henry shut his eyes. "They tell us, sir," he had boldly proclaimed, "that we are weak, unable to cope with so formidable an adversary. But when shall we be stronger?"

Now he knew—when they had allies standing by their side. Allies, while in America's favor, had not yet been secured. Henry's eyelids flung open. "But we can offer American trade to France as an inducement for their aid."

The general stood erect. "By procrastinating, our ruin is inevitable. Should we wait for formal negotiations, a whole year will pass over our heads. In the meantime, we are to struggle through the campaign without arms, ammunitions, or any necessities of war. Soldiers and officers alike will become so disappointed that they will abandon their colors, perhaps never to return. What do you believe our chances of victory under such conditions?"

Henry's mind raced, but he allowed the general's words to find a place for further study.

"But there is another consideration." The general drilled his gaze into Henry. "The spirit of the people cries for this declaration. A man of your excellent discernment need not be told how dangerous it would be, in our present circumstances, to dally with or disappoint the expectations of the bulk of the people."

Henry nodded.

The general aimed his feet toward the front hall, then turned back to Henry. "I pray, dear sir, that you may not merely present your resolution for independence to the Virginia Convention, but that you will also press upon your servants in Congress to embrace such a measure which is so necessary to our salvation."

"You have given me much to think about, and I am forever grateful." Henry stood in silence, then allowed one more argument to be spoken. The main battle of the day, the opening of Virginia's Fifth Convention, still lie before him. "But timing aside, my colony's moderation, falsely called, hath brought us to the edge of ruin. If those who have advised us until now are allowed to continue to guide us, I fear our fate will be sealed."

Pendleton scanned the faces of the hundred and twenty-eight men seated in the House chamber as they awaited the results of the vote. The day had already been marked as one of historical significance when forty-five burgesses met, and rather than adjourn, they decided to let that body die. The longest serving legislative body in the New World, more than a hundred and fifty years old, was no more. Virginia's Convention would continue to carry the baton of the now-defunct system of government, the one in which he had served for one score and four years. The legislative body which, for so many years, had carried on the affairs of Virginia in the place where he now sat.

How could the room he had come to know and love seem so foreign on this day? A double row of benches ran down the length of the room on each side. At one end, the second row curved behind the president's chair, each two small steps above the main floor, which housed a large table and small stool for the clerk. Behind the upper row, three round windows provided light, with a larger window on either side of the trio. Above the door at the other end of the room hung Virginia's coat of arms. Flanking one side, a large portrait of Queen Charlotte hung. And on the other, a portrait of King George III. The latter, an ominous reminder of the one with whom some desired to fight and with whom others desired to make peace.

Chatter pulled his attention to those who sat encircled around the chamber's floor. His distant cousin, a youthful twenty-five years old, conversed with another of the new delegates. If James Madison's namesake were anything like his father, Virginia would be in good hands for many years to come.

Pendleton exchanged glances with Bland. Now wrought with age, his longtime colleague had nominated him as president of this convention, citing the undeniable proofs of Pendleton's abilities and integrity. Despite Bland's aged body, he had stood by Pendleton through many previous battles, and he stood with him now.

Tapping toes and bouncing legs of other delegates confirmed they shared his concerns. Who would lead Virginia's most significant convention into the next phase, and how would their selection impact the future? Not only of their colony, but also of the other twelve? Had Pendleton's perceived treatment of Henry during the previous months been too much for the convention to overlook? Would the other man they had nominated, Richard Henry Lee's brother Thomas, take over the reins at this critical juncture?

The door swung open as Pendleton fingered the acceptance speech in his pocket. A speech at the outset of a convention, reminiscent of those the governor would give to the burgesses at the beginning of a session, had not yet been utilized. But with so much disagreement as to what direction this convention should go, Pendleton, if elected, must utilize every ounce of experience he could muster. Would the speech go unused?

"Gentlemen." The clerk rapped on the table in the middle of the chamber. "Gentlemen, if I could have your attention." A hush fell over the room. "The votes have been tallied."

Pendleton sat unflinching, ready to accept the will of his colleagues. He dared not look at Henry or any of his faction.

"Colonel Pendleton . . ."

The silence was deafening.

". . . has been elected to serve as president of Virginia's Fifth Convention."

Many of the strained faces in the room relaxed. Pendleton had no time to collect himself before Messrs. Bland and Cary whisked him off to the black walnut chair reserved for the body's presiding officer. The towering, yet simple, piece of furniture—which had almost eluded him on this day—was once again his.

Pendleton turned toward the delegates in his customary manner, polite and dignified, while seeking to contain the war of the ages that had just been fought within. Years of dignity and calm, provided to him by his Maker, had carried him through. He pulled his prepared remarks from his pocket.

"Gentlemen, be pleased to accept my sincere thanks for the honor done me in your election to this high and important office." His body tingled as a flood of unworthiness swept over him. "I assure you of my unremitted attention to the arduous duties of my appointment, which I will endeavor to execute with the utmost impartiality. Conscious of my want of abilities, I shall rely on your candor to provide your interpretation of all my actions."

Needing but a few peeks at his notes, Pendleton mentioned the various matters needing their attention. All without a single word regarding independence. His gaze moved around the room until he was certain every ear was attentive to his words. "Permit me to recommend calmness, unanimity, and diligence as the most likely means of bringing these items to a happy and prosperous outcome."

Pendleton nodded to the men, then brought the meeting to adjournment. It was time to prepare for the real battles that lie ahead.

Pendleton sat among the other delegates in the House chamber, fingering the document in his waistcoat pocket. Eight days had passed since he secured his position as president of the convention. Yet on this day, the delegates chose to temporarily entrust the chair to Colonel Archibald Cary, as presiding officer of the Committee of the Whole, in order to free Pendleton to participate more fully in the debate. How would it play out? Who would be counted among the victors? And who would go down in defeat?

Cary called the meeting to order and took care of preliminary business. With other matters out of the way, everyone knew what remained —the question of independence. Pendleton pulled lightly at his collar as he surveyed the House chamber. More than a hundred had gathered. Patrick Henry sat on the upper row behind the chair that Cary now occupied.

"Colonel Nelson"—Cary nodded toward the delegate from York County—"the floor is yours."

Although believed to be firmly in Henry's camp, Thomas Nelson Jr.'s popularity spanned the Virginia colony. He lifted himself from the bench and stepped into the room's center, his heels clicking against the floor. He surveyed his audience. "Gentlemen, as you are aware, the humble petitions which Philadelphia sent to our Motherland have been rejected and treated with contempt. Not only is Great Britain making every preparation to crush us, which their internal strength and foreign alliances afford them, but they are using every art to draw in the Indians and even our own slaves to take up arms against us."

Nelson paused, as if to ensure everyone's full attention. "Furthermore, Great Britain's king, by a long series of oppressive acts, has proven himself a tyrant instead of the protector of the people. We, the representatives of the colony of Virginia, do declare that we hold ourselves *absolved* of our allegiance to the Crown of Great Britain."

Pendleton stole a quick glance at the king's portrait and braced himself for Nelson's concluding remarks.

"'Resolved,'" Nelson read from the paper he had placed in front of him, "'that our delegates in Congress procure an immediate, clear, and full declaration of independency.'"

Nelson took his seat, and Henry stood. A chuckle threatened to escape Pendleton's lips. So, Henry had indeed been behind Nelson's proposal. They were acting in tandem.

"Gentlemen," Henry said, "I believe Colonel Nelson has provided us with a most reasonable resolution, yet a cause for which the lives and fortunes of our people are at stake must not be carried by mere eloquence. Such power can stimulate a people only so long."

The many times Henry had depended on eloquence to carry the day raced through Pendleton's mind. Had the young man matured in his thinking in the face of unspeakable circumstances? Or merely from age?

"Yet the spirit of the people has come to me as a spirit of fire," Henry's tone climbed in typical fashion, "and the time has come for us to untie the knot which has bound us to our Motherland." Henry aimed a broad smile in Nelson's direction. "I throw my entire support behind Colonel Nelson's resolves and do hereby second the measure."

"Hear, hear," a few of Henry's supporters cried.

Cary pushed himself from the chair and to his feet. "Gentlemen, with the gravity of the matter before us, no vote shall be taken until additional proposals have been made and debated."

Pendleton's friend and longtime member of the conservative faction, Robert C. Nicholas, rose. Yet today, each man had to shine a light upon his own soul and speak accordingly.

"Gentlemen," Nicholas said, "we have spent many months debating whether or not we were ready for war, which declaring our independence would most certainly bring to us. The answer has always been a resounding 'No' and, I dare say, is still thus. Has our army gained enough experience in such a short time to change our minds? What of the difficulty in obtaining supplies or support from France or Spain? And to the topic of our own government. We have none but what we have known and depend upon. The very one from whom we now want to declare our independence?"

For years, Pendleton had used these very arguments in debate. Yet Great Britain's behavior in recent months had negated any argument on her behalf. Was it time to walk away from the Motherland he had sought to defend for so long?

"Are we ready to provoke a war even beyond what we have already seen? Gentlemen, I say 'No.' I do not believe I am alone in doubting our preparedness for such a battle." Nicholas caught Pendleton's eye, then dropped to his seat. But all Pendleton offered was a single nod.

Others argued both for and against, while Pendleton sat in silence. A peace accompanied the benefit he had earned through seniority, the benefit of hearing others before revealing his own thoughts.

"Mr. Smith." Cary nodded to the representative from Essex County.

Meriwether Smith stood. "Gentlemen, allow me to make a proposal that goes no further than necessary."

Curiosity tickled Pendleton's mind. Had the scales tilted for planters of Tidewater, or would they keep the conservative stance needed to protect their vulnerable location from Britain's attack?

"'Resolved,'" Smith read from the paper he held in his hands, "'that the government of this colony be dissolved and that a committee be appointed to prepare a declaration of rights, rather than of independency—a plan of government to maintain peace and order, thus securing substantial and equal liberty to the people.'"

Who could blame the Tidewater for their conservative position? Would that this resolve was enough. But the convention must come together and speak for all Virginians, not just one region. Pendleton furrowed his brow.

Could an answer be found that would satisfy all?

Somehow, it must.

Pendleton surveyed the faces of the hundred and twelve men seated around the perimeter of the House chamber. The various views that had been presented each found a place in his mind, then he motioned to the presiding officer.

Cary turned his focus toward his friend. "Colonel Edmund Pendleton of Caroline County."

CHAPTER 23

All In

May 14 - 17, 1776

"Thank you, Mr. Chairman." Pendleton stood, providing a weary smile for his colleagues seated around the House chamber. "Gentlemen, while opinions among us are diverse and loyalties run deep, if ever there was a time for thoughtfulness to prevail, 'tis now."

Pendleton took two steps into the center of the room, pivoted to those behind him, then swept his arm toward his fellow delegates. "We extend our thanks to those gentlemen who have provided us with their thoughts during such a trying time. Dare I say that each word spoken contains elements worthy of our consideration. Not only would going too far or practicing too much constraint seal our doom, but doing either in the wrong manner would produce the same results."

The eyes of the men surrounding him reflected the weight of the battle they had endured—a battle of the minds. Lines etched deep upon each face. Many leaned forward, locked on every word their senior statesman had to offer. Others gazed into nothingness, lost for a moment in their own reflections before turning their attention back to him.

"May I be so bold," Pendleton said, "as to provide a means of divorcing ourselves from the tyrannical practices under which we have lived for more than a decade, yet place the responsibility of our actions at the feet of those to whom it rightly belongs. At the feet of our oppressors.

"Gentlemen, nearly a decade ago, Parliament usurped unlimited authority to bind their American colonies in all cases whatsoever. And the British Ministry has attempted to execute its many tyrannical acts in the most inhuman and cruel manner. In addition, and listen to me closely, King George III himself has withdrawn his protection from the said colonies. And, jointly with the Ministry and Parliament, he has begun and is now pursuing, with the utmost violence, a barbarous war against us. This violates every civil and religious right."

Pendleton bowed his head, letting the weight of the moment sink in, then pulled the document from his waistcoat pocket.

"'Resolved, therefore,'" he read, "'that the union that has hitherto subsisted between Great Britain and the American colonies is thereby *already* dissolved, and that the inhabitants of this colony are *already* discharged from any allegiance to the Crown of Great Britain.'" Pendleton's heart raced. "Gentlemen, we have no need to threaten to untie the knot with our Motherland, for *they* have already done so." He gave a solemn nod to his colleagues, then returned to his seat.

Mentally spent, yet satisfied, he had settled the battle within.

A brief debate ensued over specific items in Pendleton's resolves. In the end, the convention placed its confidence in the one who had always managed to find a path forward.

"Colonel Pendleton," Cary said, "the convention does hereby charge you to prepare a final resolution, which we will review and debate tomorrow."

The weight of the world settled on Pendleton's shoulders, and he closed his eyes in prayer. *Please, God, help me.*

The bread and cheese that one of the Randolph servants had brought to Pendleton's room sat untouched. Never had the home felt so empty. While his every need had been met with generosity and grace, Pendleton longed for one more evening to converse with his old friend, almost seven months in the grave. Pendleton rose from the desk, carried his plate to the table, then drifted to the window.

Slaves milled about the courtyard attending to late evening chores while reflections of his personal journey turned over in his mind. Past losses, and nearly losing Sarah two years before, seemed distant now. While scars remained, the sharpest pains had dulled with the passage of time.

He glanced back at the paper and quill. What he penned tonight would not only change his path, but also the path of every American colonist. He turned back to the window, mulling over the arguments of the day. Arguments years in the making.

Petition after petition laid before the king had been met with rejection and scorn. The Motherland had pushed away the colonists' desire for a peaceful resolution. Worse, she declared her colonies to be in a state of rebellion, removed any protection, and took up arms against them.

Even so, the American colonies did not stand ready to fight against the most powerful force in the world. In a reasonable mind, the lack of a trained army, foreign allies, and their own form of government screamed for more time to prepare.

Yet the enemy had come against them with weapons in hand. Lexington, Concord, Great Bridge, and Norfolk could no longer be considered anomalies. They formed a pattern of hatred and mistrust—confirmation that Great Britain believed blows must decide whether the colonies were to remain subject to her or become independent.

No longer could the colonies depend on reason alone to guide them. Now they must trust in the spirit of the people, as Patrick Henry had championed for so many years.

Submission to a tyrant. Or fight to be free.

No other alternative remained.

Pendleton returned to the blank piece of paper on the desk, organized his notes from the day, and reached for the quill. United they would stand or divided they would fall, but all as Americans.

No matter the cost.

The next day, Pendleton made his way down the Capitol steps amid thank-yous and pats on the back from the hundred men pouring out of the building with him. Despite the limited time he'd had to write the document, the convention unanimously approved Pendleton's resolves. Even Henry had come aboard before Nicholas. No one received everything he wanted, yet everyone seemed to appreciate Pendleton's efforts to find the common ground.

"Down with the old!" a voice shouted from above.

The representatives exchanged looks of confusion, then hurried into the courtyard where they turned to see the source of the commotion. Pendleton found his footing, then looked up.

Something caught in his chest.

Two men, standing on the platform which encircled the building's cupola, were lowering the British flag. The time had come to say farewell to old loyalties—loyalties which the British flag symbolized.

Goodbyes never came easy for Pendleton, yet so much had brought him, his colony, and his country to this moment. Perhaps King Solomon was right.

To everything there is a season,
and a time to every purpose under the heaven:
a time to mourn, and a time to dance . . .
a time to keep, and a time to cast away . . .
a time for peace . . . and a time for war.

Pendleton bowed his head. *Lord, please give strength and grace to those who are left behind.*

"Colonel Pendleton?" The voice pulled him back from his ponderings. A lad, no more than fourteen, held out an upturned hat already half filled with paper money. An earnest expression filled his freckled face.

"Yes?"

The boy raised the hat an inch or two. "Sir, we're taking up a collection for the ceremony sure to come and would appreciate any—"

Pendleton held up his palm. Although his leadership roles and aging body would prevent him from being able to take up arms, he could still donate to the cause. "Please drop by the Randolph home later today so that I might make a more substantial donation."

"Much obliged, sir." The lad flashed a face-splitting grin, then scampered away.

Pendleton's attention returned to the merriment unfolding about him. Bells tolled while artillery and small arms discharged. Troops emerged to join in the celebration. He cast an encouraging smile in their direction. Some would give their lives as a sacrificial gift for a cause greater than themselves. A heartfelt thank-you formed on his lips as they slipped by.

Henry lifted his glass in toast to America's independent states, to the Grand Congress, and to General Washington. Each toast set off another round of artillery fire and cheers by the throng gathered at Waller's

Grove. Henry caught glimpses of Pendleton who, along with others of the Committee of Safety, had completed his inspection of the troops. Members of the convention mingled with the city's inhabitants, as each celebrated the passing of Pendleton's resolves from the day before. Shouts of joy, laughter, and applause filled the air.

Henry leapt onto a nearby tree stump, raising his glass high. "Huzzah!" he shouted. Years of frustration melted away amid Virginia's decision to push the colonies toward independence.

The grove, situated just east of the Capitol, had served as home to some of his former soldiers and brought back a flood of memories. Logs surrounded a nearby campfire on which some of the troops sat, meat sizzling atop the blaze. The late spring breeze also carried the scent of gunpowder. Although Henry's time with the troops had been brief, he was grateful for it. Now, as a civilian, he had reclaimed his place of influence. Words and the ability to inspire others acted as his artillery.

Pendleton's unifying words, which the convention had adopted and were now being read aloud to the soldiers, brought Henry a renewed sense of appreciation for the differing roles each played. He turned his attention to the town crier as he moved toward the end of Pendleton's resolves.

"'Wherefore,'" the crier read, "'appealing to the searcher of our hearts for the sincerity of former declarations, expressing our desire to preserve a connection with that nation, and that we are driven from that inclination by their wicked and the eternal laws of self-preservation . . .'"

Henry raised both hands and motioned for everyone around him to listen to the words flowing from the town crier's lips.

"'Resolved unanimously, that the delegates appointed to represent this colony in General Congress be instructed to propose to that respectable body to declare the United Colonies free and independent states, absolved from all allegiance to, or dependence upon, the Crown or Parliament of Great Britain.'"

"Hurrah!" Henry shouted above the roar of the crowd, then turned to Pendleton with a gentleman's bow. He straightened and shouted for all to hear. "Thank you, Colonel Pendleton, for your most gracious contribution to our beloved American colonies."

He threw his fist heavenward. "Hip, hip!"

"Huzzah!" the reply came.

Pendleton tilted his head in acknowledgement.

Although he had used less insistent language than in Nelson and Henry's resolves, *propose* rather than *procure*, Henry's desire for separation would be conveyed. He had cast his vote to accept the resolves. Perhaps Pendleton's softer tone would bring the colonies together in a way that Henry's spirited nature had not been able to do in ten years. In the end, Virginia's delegation in Philadelphia would receive instructions to propose that Congress declare independence—the very thing for which Henry had fought for so long.

The building now empty, Pendleton sat in the pew box of Williamsburg's parish church, reflecting on all that had transpired. Artillery smoke from the previous day's festivities had drifted away. The building's cream-colored walls and pew boxes, accented with stained wood trim, provided a sense of calm amid the new realities. Demonstrations of joy and the candles that illuminated the town the night before had given way to a day of fasting and prayer that Congress had declared two months earlier. The opening words of that declaration, "In times of impending calamity and distress," echoed the sentiments of many.

Pendleton's prayers turned to kinfolk whose lives were on the line. They were good men, and ready to continue the fight.

And what of John Penn? He would be part of the Congress who would debate Virginia's proposal. If the men gathered in Philadelphia accepted it and America lost its fight, Britain would certainly fit Penn's neck for a hangman's noose.

The passage chosen by the convention's chaplain brought comfort. "Be not afraid, nor dismayed, by reason of this great multitude; for the battle is not yours, but God's."

Pendleton nodded. No matter his position or abilities, it would take the hand of the Lord to keep his loved ones safe. And if God chose to take any of them home to glory, so be it—for the sake of the cause. The colonists would fight, and some would surely die, so that America could be free.

AFTERWORD

SUMMER 1776 AND BEYOND

The road to freedom was long and arduous. Lasting more than eight years, the war took the lives of twenty-five thousand American soldiers. Liberty came at a high price, even for those who survived.

After signing the Declaration of Independence, John Penn continued to serve in Congress until 1780. In 1777, he signed the first constitution of the United States, known as the Articles of Confederation.

North Carolina, Penn's adopted state, played a significant role in the war, with Jefferson referring to the October 1780 Battle of Kings Mountain as "the turn of the tide of success." Penn served on North Carolina's Board of War, formed in early September of the same year. At times, he faithfully carried the bulk of the load for the three-member committee until his health would no longer allow it. In July 1781, he declined his appointment to the governor's council, citing his ill state of health. By 1783, he no longer served in politics. He died in

1788 at forty-seven years old. Many believe his grueling travels to and from Philadelphia may have contributed to his early death.

A monument stands at his old homeplace near Stovall, North Carolina. Another, at Guilford Courthouse National Military Park, stands in memory of Hewes, Hooper, and Penn, where the remains of the latter two were reinterred in 1894.

At the close of the war, Penn's daughter, Lucy, married Jack, better known as John Taylor of Caroline. His lucrative law practice allowed him to purchase land, and the couple settled at Hazelwood, a plantation about ten miles from Jack's surrogate father and lifelong mentor, Edmund Pendleton.

Although Taylor served multiple terms, both elected and appointed, in Virginia's House of Delegates (1779-1800) and the United States Senate (1792-1824), agriculture became his passion. In 1818, his book of agricultural essays became among the first to be published on that subject in America. A staunch defender of self-government and states' rights, he also wrote multiple books on political thought between 1794 and 1823. One British political scientist of the twentieth and twenty-first centuries referred to Taylor as "the most impressive political theorist that America ever produced."

Taylor died at home on August 20, 1824. Taylor County, West Virginia, was named in his honor.

Many other Pendletons and Taylors served as military officers during the Revolutionary War. The Old Pendleton District of South Carolina (now Pickens, Oconee, and Anderson Counties) was named for Edmund's nephew, Judge Henry Pendleton, one of Nathaniel's minutemen sons.

December 1776 found William Woodford and his Virginia regiment heading to New Jersey to join Washington's army. When Virginia's regiments reorganized early in 1777, Congress appointed Woodford as brigadier general. Woodford and his men were involved in the Battle of Brandywine Creek in September 1777 and the Battle of Germantown in October of the same year.

Other battles followed. Then, in December 1779, they were ordered to go to Charleston, South Carolina, as reinforcements to the Southern Continental Army. The eight-hundred-mile march, during what became the harshest winter of the war, took its toll on Woodford's troops. Those who survived the trip arrived in Charleston on April 7, 1780. General Henry Clinton, the British commander in chief, and his men had arrived in February and surrounded the city. Although the arrival of Woodford and his men provided a fresh confidence to those in the garrison, the British two-to-one advantage proved to be too much to overcome. On May 12, the commander of America's southern troops surrendered more than five thousand troops, their officers, and equipment. The largest loss of the war. The British shipped Woodford to New York aboard a prison ship where, six months later, he died of disease. He was buried with full miliary honors at New York's Trinity Church.

Lord Dunmore left Virginia for New York in the summer of 1776, more than a year after fleeing the palace in Williamsburg. He later returned to Britain where he continued to receive his governor's pay until the Motherland recognized America's independence. Reelected to the House of Lords, he sailed to Virginia with the goal of recapturing it. While at sea, however, he heard of the surrender of Cornwallis and sailed to New York instead. From 1787 to 1796, he governed in the Bahamas, where Loyalists received land grants. He died in England in 1809.

In 1776, the newly-formed state of Virginia selected Patrick Henry as their governor. He served three consecutive one-year terms and again from 1784 to 1786. Despite Henry's best efforts to keep intact the powers once held by the royal governor, the House stripped away many of them prior to giving that role to Henry. He married Dorothea Spotswood Dandridge in 1777 and sold his Scotchtown home where difficult memories remained.

As key spokesman for the Anti-Federalists, Henry chose to exercise his influence as a representative to Virginia's House of Delegates. In battles over the United States Constitution, he fought hard against Federalists, such as James Madison, yet lost. Upon defeat, he committed to being "a peaceable citizen" while claiming "my head, my hand, and my heart shall be at liberty to retrieve the loss of liberty and remove the defects of that system—in a constitutional way."

His popularity and influence continued in Virginia's House of Delegates until he retired from that body in 1790. He returned to his law practice where his gift of persuasion kept him in high demand. Henry declined appointments as the federal Secretary of State, Attorney General, Justice of the Supreme Court, and minister to Spain and France. With Washington's encouragement, however, Henry reentered politics and won back his seat in the state legislature. Before he was able to take office, he died at his Red Hill home on June 6, 1799, having fathered seventeen children and a legacy which lives on.

In the spring of 1776, Edmund Pendleton received letters from Thomas Jefferson pleading for Pendleton to do his best to keep Jefferson from being reelected to Congress. Jefferson desired to be in Virginia where he could be part of forming the new government and make a difference. Pendleton's efforts failed, and Jefferson returned to Philadelphia where Congress tapped him to write the Declaration of Independence.

In October 1776, under the state's new constitution, Pendleton chaired Virginia's House of Delegates, the successor to the House of Burgesses and Virginia's Conventions. The month must have been bittersweet, as Pendleton's longtime friend Richard Bland collapsed on the streets of Williamsburg while serving as one of the delegates in the new government. Bland died later that day. His death left Pendleton as Virginia's longest-serving representative.

Elected by the assembly to revise Virginia's laws, Pendleton, Jefferson, Mason, George Wythe, and Thomas Ludwell Lee met in January 1777 to begin the laborious process. Mason, citing he was no lawyer, asked to be excused. Lee became ill and died three months later, placing the responsibility in the laps of the three who remained.

Two months later, Pendleton fell from a horse, resulting in a dislocated hip, dependence on crutches until his death, and plenty of time to work on the revision of Virginia's laws. Thirsty for news, Pendleton found refreshment in letters Richard Henry Lee sent to him while serving in Congress. Woodford and Jack kept Pendleton abreast of news from the warfront.

Despite the condition of their beloved representative, Caroline County reelected Pendleton as a delegate to Virginia's House. With Pendleton unable to attend the May 1777 session, the House appointed another to lead them, promising to have Pendleton step back into that role once he was able. He never returned to that position, and made plans to retire from more than forty years in public service.

A servant at heart, however, he could not refuse pleas from his colleagues to become a judge in the newly-formed High Court of Chancery in 1777, then to serve as president of the Supreme Court of Appeals beginning in 1779. When Virginia's Convention ratified the

Constitution of the United States in 1788, Pendleton served as its leader by unanimous consent.

Very few can claim the reach that Pendleton had during his lifetime. He served as Virginia's leader in each branch of government. First, as the president of the Committee of Safety in 1775 and 1776—effectively the governor while none served as such. Then as Speaker of two conventions in the same years. And finally, as the leader of Virginia's Court of Appeals from 1779 until his death. As the first president of the United States, George Washington appointed Edmund Pendleton as a judge for the United States District of Virginia, but Pendleton declined due to his advancing age. In 1799, Thomas Jefferson and Jack Taylor persuaded Pendleton to write a pamphlet which proved to be of considerable importance to Jefferson's presidential campaign of 1800. Americans elected Jefferson to be their third president, after John Adams had served as their second. James Madison, Jr. became the fourth.

In July 1803, at eighty-one years old, Pendleton wrote to Jack Taylor to explain why he and his wife would need to delay a promised visit to Hazelwood. Extreme heat and sickness pervaded their neighborhood. Three months later, Pendleton arrived late to the court's fall term, likely due to illness or age. Ever true to his desire to serve the people, however, he arrived in Richmond, Virginia's capital since 1780, to wrap up his duties before retirement.

On October 25, 1803, he conducted business as usual, then returned to the Swan Tavern for the night after dining with Virginia's governor. The next day, word arrived at the court that Pendleton had taken ill. At four o'clock, they received word of his death. (At the time of this publication, several sources and Pendleton's gravestone, incorrectly list October 23 as his date of death. Minutes from Virginia's Supreme Court of Appeals, October 24 thru 29, 1803, along with various newspaper clippings, clearly indicated October 26,1803, as his date of death.)

Virginia's court declared two months of mourning. Both the governor's council in Virginia and the United States House of Representatives in Washington, D.C., declared a month of mourning. When the country's Senate reconvened, it took similar action for both Pendleton and Samuel Adams, who had also died in October. Both men lived twenty years beyond the official end to the Revolutionary War.

In Richmond, Pendleton's body lay in state in the Hall of Virginia's House of Delegates before six pallbearers ushered him from the chamber for one last time. Among the six was one of Patrick Henry's sons-in-law, Spencer Roane, the youngest member of the court. Another pallbearer and member of the court, Peter Lyons, had worked with Pendleton for many years. Now he would have to bear alone the responsibility of the Robinson Estate, already forty years in the probate. First buried at his beloved Edmundsbury, Pendleton's body was reinterred to the Bruton Parish Church in Williamsburg in 1907.

West Virginia and Kentucky each named a county in honor of Edmund Pendleton.

Shortly before his death, Pendleton wrote a short autobiography in which he exclaimed, "Not unto me! Not unto me, O Lord, but unto thy name, be praise."

On April 11, 1828, Pendleton's reflections on his life appeared in the Richmond *Enquirer*. The explanatory heading that preceded his words included an admonition to young people who aspired for public honors and advancement: Read Pendleton's biography and "follow on in his slow, steady, useful and brilliant cause."

As one who had the privilege to compose an account of Pendleton's life, I can only add a hearty "Amen!" Find the path God has for you, then follow it with all your heart.

Whether this [independence] will prove to be a blessing or a curse,
will depend upon the use our people make of the blessings which a
gracious God hath bestowed on us. If they are wise, they will be great
and happy. If they are of a contrary character, they will be miserable.
Righteousness alone can exalt them as a nation. Reader: whoever thou
art, remember this, & in thy sphere, practice virtue thyself,
& encourage it in others.

—Patrick Henry

Acknowledgements

Even a second novel, especially one filled with history, can be a huge undertaking. Many heartfelt thanks to those who contributed to its accuracy and to those who helped turn it into a story worthy of a reader's time and attention.

I am especially grateful to Anne Conkling—historian, public speaker, and tour guide—whom I met at Bruton Parish Church in 2011 while vacationing in Williamsburg, Virginia. Her knowledge and love of Edmund Pendleton convinced me his story deserved to be told.

Those who aided in my formal research:

• Gerald Underdown, Richard Shumann, and others who not only bring the characters of this novel to life on the cobblestone streets of Colonial Williamsburg, but also graciously entertained the multitude of questions I brought to them during my research trips.
• Tami Shumann, who provided an enormous amount of feedback and information, both priceless.
• Patrick Henry Jolly, a descendant of his namesake through two of his children, who graciously offered input despite the differences between our respective ancestors. I look forward to the four of us sitting down in heaven one day to sort it all out.
• Mark Pace, specialist for the North Carolina Room at the Granville County Library, who provided me with materials about John Penn and loves learning about him as much as I do.

• Christian Higgins, Archivist and Library Manager at the
Independence National Historical Park in Philadelphia.
• Melissa C. Schutt and others at Williamsburg's John D.
Rockefeller Jr. Library who pointed me to a wealth of information.
• Caitlin Curtis Olsen, Director of Education and Donor Systems,
who allowed me access to Red Hill Patrick Henry National
Memorial library.
• Ethan Purita of Red Hill Patrick Henry National Memorial.
• Kimberly Sholar, staff at the Orange County Public Library in
Hillsborough, North Carolina, who uncovered several key resources
to aid in my research.
• Staff at Historic St. John's Church who help keep the "Liberty or
Death" speech alive.
• Kristal Murphey who provided a very informative tour of Historic
Halifax in North Carolina.
• Barbara Valdes, branch manager of Halifax County Library in
North Carolina, who aided me in my research.
• Nancy Stewart, Site Supervisor at Guilford Courthouse National
Military Park, for her help during one of my early research trips.
• Sarah K. Myers, Access Services Librarian at Mount Vernon, who
pointed me to various resources.
• Archives References Services at the Library of Virginia at
Richmond, who provided me with documentation I needed in
order to determine Edmund Pendleton's date of death.

Professionals and readers who helped turn my research into more
than a brain dump:

• Beta readers, whose feedback on a less-than-perfect draft helped
make the story shine. I owe an extra measure of praise to Paul
Hansil, who did a second read-through of my manuscript, and to

Dottie Molineaux, who helped sort out Edmund Pendleton's date of death.
• Isabella Skellenger, whose amazing insights and red pen took the story to a whole new level.
• Others who found i's that needed dots and t's that needed crossing.

Writers, knowing both the trials and triumphs of our crazy journey, contributed to making this novel many times better than it would have been without them:

• Members of my American Christian Fiction Writers group, notably Christine Boatwright, Isabella Skellenger, Katie (and Andy) Foth, Austin Finley, Debby Young, and Keith Hoffman.
• Members of the Word Weavers International chapters of which I was a part, especially the Page 53 and Hendersonville, North Carolina, chapters who helped push me over the finish line. A special thanks to Jenifer Jennings and Fred von Kamecke.
• Other writing friends who have been part of this amazing journey.

As with my first novel, my husband deserves the biggest thanks. Without his support, this story would never have seen the light of day.

For additional information and resources,
please visit
cammolineux.com.